Orchestra

Heather Osborne

What happens when the protégé becomes the maestro?

Copyright 2018
by Heather Osborne

This is a work of fiction. Names, characters, places, and incidents are either the product of the author's imagination or used fictitiously and any resemblance to actual people, alive or dead, business, establishments, locales, or events is entirely coincidental.

Any reference to real events, businesses, or organizations is intended to give the fiction a sense of realism and authenticity.

All rights reserved. No part of this publication may be reproduced, stored in a retrieval system, or transmitted by any means—electronic, mechanical, photographic (photocopying), recording or otherwise—without prior permission in writing from the author.

ISBN: 9781717933416

Cover Design by Heather Osborne
Editing by Susie Watson

Dedication

To my son, Alex, who shows great patience beyond his years while Mommy is working.
Love, love

Prelude

Tchaikovsky's *Valzer dei Fiori* whispered from the inset speakers in his study. He hummed along, eyes tracing back and forth across the papers on his desk. A quick flourish of his pen added his signature to the bottom of one of the documents. He leaned back, sighing with satisfaction, replacing the silver-inlaid pen back in its holder. He carefully removed a narrow cigar from the silver case perched to the side of his spotless desk.

Rising, he straightened his Armani suit jacket and crossed the room to a cherry-wood bookcase. Sliding *Les Misérables* from its place, he keyed in a code using the concealed number pad. With a gentle whoosh, the bookcase slid aside. He crossed the threshold, descending into the corridor put in place by his grandfather. The bookcase closed behind him. The music faded, but he continued to hum the tune, twirling the cigar in his fingers. The score would be hitting the pinnacle movements shortly.

He came to another steel-enforced door, running his hand over the cool metal. Retinal scans, as well as a carefully placed fingerprint confirmed his identity. The door retracted, secreting into the side wall. As before, he stepped into the well-lit room, the fluorescent bulbs having been triggered by a sensor pad on the floor.

Moving to the nearby table, he stripped off his jacket and loosened his tie. The cigar would make for a suitable reward afterward. He slipped into a white jumpsuit, much like a painter would wear. He could not risk the contamination of his clothing. Snapping on latex gloves, he placed a mask over his face. He picked up a hypodermic needle and carefully filled it from one of several vials on the shelf next to the table. The yellow tinged liquid rushed up inside the glass tube, the air bubbles subsiding after a few flicks.

He walked over to a bound figure in the center of the room, his shoes muted by the booties of the suit. Holzer, his face concealed by a black cloth bag, began to struggle violently—thrashing—even though the chair was firmly bolted to the floor. His naked chest heaved with silent sobs. "Please…"

Grasping Holzer's arm firmly, the man jabbed the needle in, depressing the plunger. Immediately, Holzer began to twitch, hoarse screams emanating from beneath the bag. The acid ate a gaping hole in Holzer's flesh, and the screams subsided to whimpers, then silence. The man set the syringe aside and pressed two fingers to Holzer's carotid artery. After a few moments, he found a faint sign of life. He smiled.

Part One

Exposition

1

Dr. Lindsay Young peered at the patient before her, knowing there was little hope of her words bringing comfort to the family crowded around the bedside. The ten-year-old girl, hooked up to several monitors and a life support machine, was dying. Her small body had been too badly damaged. She checked the girl's vitals, trying to avoid looking at the battered face of the child.

According to Detective Gregory Shaw, they had found her in an abandoned warehouse belonging to her stepfather. She had been raped and beaten. There were no suspects in the case. The mother wept openly, as her husband's arm encompassed her shoulders. He had been cleared, having been on a hunting trip out of state with two of his brothers. It was one of the most brutal cases Lindsay had ever seen in her years in the Intensive Care Unit at Lakeland Hospital in the heart of Palo Alto, California.

Leaving the family to consider their options, she slipped from the room, almost bumping into Shaw, his otherwise rugged handsome face showing the ravages of the case. She felt a small spark of attraction for the man, but as he was married, she kept her distance. No way was she going down that path.

"How is she? Is there any hope?"

Lindsay shook her head, brow creasing. "There's nothing more we can do for her. The internal injuries were too severe. The family..." Her voice caught, and she motioned to the small staff breakroom.

Shaw trailed after, his eyes flitting back to the closed door, muffled sobs coming from the interior. "Yes?" he pressed, once they were safely ensconced in the room.

"The family has decided to turn off life support and let her find peace." Lindsay didn't believe in God, but she felt sometimes allowing a person to pass and escape the pain was the best way. Moving to the coffee pot, she flipped it on, taking down two mugs at Shaw's nod.

"Shit. This isn't what I wanted to happen. Corrine is the only link to our killer. We are at a dead end." He raked his fingers through his graying brown hair. No doubt it was the strain of so many homicide cases which had added the ashen color to the strands.

The pot beeped, and Lindsay handed him a steaming mug. "I know. I feel somewhat at a loss as well. I wish there was more I could do."

"You kept her alive, so her family could say goodbye. That's sometimes more than enough in these cases."

Lindsay thought to her own towheaded little boy, Taylor. The five-year-old brought light to her dim life, reminding her there were better things in this world to look to. "I suppose."

"There's no supposing about it, Linds. You did good."

The pair sipped their coffee in retrospective silence. She had gotten to know Shaw rather well over the passing years, even if most of his cases' victims never made it through her doors. Sometimes, she wished it were that way all the time. Seeing people suffer because of the actions of others revolted her.

"How's Taylor?"

Lindsay blinked, not expecting him to ask, or remember. "He's good. Started kindergarten this year, so my mom gets a break from his chatter in the mornings."

"Does he like it?" Shaw fixed her with a stare, his pale blue eyes seeking anything to take his mind off the case.

"Sure, I guess. I always hear about who's gotten into trouble. He can't tell me what he's learned though, but he remembers that!" She laughed to herself. "He's something else, I tell ya."

"Kids are."

"And yours?"

"Out in Montana with Carol's folks. She wanted a vacation, but I had to...well, you know."

Lindsay didn't want to pry. She knew Shaw and his wife were on tenterhooks. It was tough being married to a detective. *Or a doctor.* "Yeah, I know."

"Anyway, I had better get going. Thanks for the coffee." He passed her the empty mug, and she set the pair in the metal sink.

As they departed the breakroom, a nurse met Lindsay with the relevant paperwork for the family. She wished this would be the end to their horror, but an autopsy needed to be carried out on the child. Even after all the medical examination, Corrine Evans would not be able to rest yet.

✳✳✳

Taylor's screams met Lindsay as she crossed the threshold of her mother's townhouse. She rubbed her aching neck and dropped her keys into the glass bowl perched on the sideboard. The familiar sound brought the ruckus to a halt. Small feet pounded down the stairs, and a blur in Spider-Man pajamas flew at her. "MAMA!" She barely managed to scoop him up.

Behind him came her mother, Sandra, blonde hair mussed. She hid her exhaustion well. "It's about time. I was ready to call in the Marines."

Taylor poked his lower lip out. "No, Gramma!" He twisted a lock of Lindsay's matching blonde hair around his finger. "She wouldn't read about the giant."

Sandra crossed her arms. "We read that one already. I told you it was one story, and then bed."

Lindsay stared down into her son's mischievous face. "Is that so?"

"Well, actually..." Taylor grinned, twin dimples appearing on his cheeks.

"That's it, mister. Scoot! I'll be up to tuck you in in a minute." She set him down and patted his butt.

"But I'm not tired!" He pouted spectacularly, as he stomped up the stairs.

When Taylor was out of earshot, Sandra's expression melted into concern. "It was that little girl, wasn't it?"

Lindsay nodded, finally able to slip out of her coat. "Yes. The family...they decided to let her pass peacefully." She knew her mother would keep anything said confidential. The woman was her rock.

Clicking her tongue, Sandra shook her head. "Poor family. I don't envy the mother, having to make such a decision." She drew Lindsay to her, hugging her tightly. "I hope they find the bastard who did this."

"Mooooommmmmy! Are you coming?" Taylor's voice came from the second floor.

"In a minute, bug." Lindsay smiled at her mother. "Tea?"

Sandra grinned back. "Yes, yes. I'll warm up some spaghetti for you. Go."

Lindsay climbed the stairs, stopping at her son's door. Soft snores issued forth from the room. She navigated a minefield of Legos, action figures, and toy trucks. It amazed her how quickly he could go from raging tornado to sleeping angel. She crouched and placed a kiss on his soft brow, breathing in the scent of the mango shampoo her mother had used on his hair.

Gathering a few bits of dirty laundry, she crossed the carpeted floor, pulling the door over. Stifling a yawn, she dropped the clothes into the basket at the top of the stairs, before the smell of spaghetti sauce drew her to the kitchen.

✱✱✱

The heels of his Tanino Crisci Lilian shoes let out a satisfying tap on the hospital linoleum. He considered them a necessary investment, much like every part of his wardrobe. The faint smell of disinfectant invaded his nostrils as he paused by the cracked door of the bereavement chapel. Inside, the family of Corrine Evans grieved the brutal death of their daughter. He peered in, leaning forward ever so slightly. Sobs emitted from the interior—a female, probably the mother.

"Pardon me, can I help you?"

He straightened, shaking his head. "Apologies. I am going to see a client."

The man held two Styrofoam cups of steaming liquid. There was a badge clipped to his belt. "Does it have to do with the Evans family?"

He shook his head, turning on a heel and moving back down the corridor. He knew the law enforcement official would be slightly dumbfounded and angered by the rude dismissal, but it was none of his concern.

Rounding a corner, he sidestepped a nurse bustling by with her head in a file and approached the reception desk. His easy smile put the pretty strawberry blonde nursing student into a tizzy. "Mr. Edward Haversham III to see a Mr. Frederick Jones."

She let forth a tittering laugh, causing him to inwardly wince. "Oh, Freddy! He's so funny! Can I ask what relation you are to Mr. Jones?"

Edward reached into his breast pocket and withdrew a gold case, from which he removed an ivory business card. "I am Mr. Jones' attorney, Brittney." He caught her name badge out of the corner of his eye.

Brittney flushed pink, clearly in awe of his evident breeding and bearing. "Oh, yes, well, I need to check with the head nurse. Can you wait here a moment?" She stood and hurried to a staff room at the end of the hall.

Edward narrowed his eyes, irritated by the delay in his appointment. He spun, leaning back against the desk, watching the oblivious people drift along the corridor.

"Mr. Haversim?" Brittney's high-pitched voice met his ears, and he inwardly winced.

"Haver*sham*. Yes?" He turned, regarding her coldly.

"Oh, sorry. Mr. Jones says he's up for visitors."

Edward retrieved his briefcase from the floor. "How *generous* of him." He made a mental note to charge double to the man's doddering father as punishment for the misuse of his time. He followed the wiggling posterior of the student in front of him.

As they rounded a corner, Brittney indicated to a door on the right. "He's in there, sir. Oh!" She handed over a sticker with a green 'V.' "You'll have to stick this to your jacket."

Edward shuddered at the thought of the residue from the cheap sticker marring his impeccable suit. He plucked it from her hand with two fingers. "As you wish. Thank you for your assistance." He breezed into the room, shutting the door in her open-mouthed face.

Freddy Jones sat up in the bed, his wrist graced with the tell-tale silver bracelets given to him by the local law enforcement agency. In the corner of the room, a uniformed officer leaned against a wall, peering back at Edward as he shut the door. "Hello, Mr. Jones. I am Edward Haversham III. I have been retained by your father to clear up this…nasty business. Officer." He nodded crisply to the bored man. "May I speak to my client in private?"

The officer studied the pair with marked suspicion. "I'll

step outside, but I have to have the door open. Orders, ya know." He checked Freddy's cuffs, before exiting the room, leaving the door ajar.

"Good evening, Mr. Jones. I hope they aren't treating you too poorly." Edward set his briefcase down on the swiveling table where Freddy would eat his sub-par hospital meals.

"Yeah, not too bad. You said Pop sent ya? Funny. I haven't seen him in years. How did he find out I was here?"

Edward clicked open the gold-plated locks. "Easily enough, I suppose. A full-scale, televised shootout with the police quite possibly tipped him off. He does still care a great deal about your well-being, Mr. Jones."

"Yeah, I guess. Lucky to get away with a bullet in my leg, huh?" He let out a laugh. "Stupid, eh? Robbing a coffee shop next to the police station. Don't know what I was thinking!"

Edward pressed his lips together, suppressing his first instinct to tell this miscreant exactly what he was thinking. The track marks gracing his arms were more than enough for him to know Freddy Jones was looking for a fix. The withdrawals were being kept at bay by medication, currently being paid for by decent citizens. He studied the plastic tubing stretching from the hanging bag.

"Ahem, regardless of your motives, you are facing some steep charges, Mr. Jones. Your father has agreed to use his influence to assist you, but he requests some collateral."

"Collater-what?" Freddy's forehead wrinkled.

"*Collateral*, Mr. Jones. He does not wish to see his investment go to waste." Edward withdrew the crisp paper from his briefcase and unscrewed the cap of his fountain pen. "He wants you to commit to a year-long rehabilitation program at an exclusive center in Colorado. Once you complete the program, and remain sober for a period of one year, he will welcome you back into his good graces, as well as provide financial support for the duration of your life. One codicil though, Mr. Jones. You must submit to weekly drug testing."

"Codi-what?"

Edward pressed down the growing need to punch this infirmed man. "Addendum, addition, postscript." He held out the paper to Freddy, twitching as he wrinkled the document when he took it. "You are welcome to think it over. I will return tomorrow for your answer." Edward snapped the leather briefcase shut, taking an indulgent moment to run a finger over the gold embossed initials. "Good day, Mr. Jones."

"Hey! Wait, Mr.…."

"Haversham. Yes?" Edward lifted the briefcase from the hospital table, allowing it to come to rest by his side.

"How is Pop?"

"Eager to provide his only son with a second chance at upholding the family name and business, Mr. Jones. If I were in your position, I would jump at this opportunity." Edward seethed internally at this rat inheriting a fortune. Still, he would receive a hefty sum himself for the few hours he would spend with the scum.

"Uh, thanks." Freddy squinted at the paper, as Edward exited the hospital room, nodding once at the waiting officer.

2

"Taylor Ellis Young, I am not going to ask you again. Come downstairs and get your shoes on! We are running late!" Lindsay gratefully accepted the travel mug of coffee from her mother, gathering up her purse and keys. "Thanks, Mom."

"I can take him, really." Sandra untucked her daughter's ponytail from the collar of her coat.

Lindsay smiled, almost giving in to the request. "I have to be maternal sometimes, even if it's only once a week. TAYLOR!"

The five-year-old bounded down the stairs, his school backpack in tow. "Mrs. Phillips stinks! And she makes us sit still for circle time, and I hate it!"

He plopped at the bottom of the stairs and reached for his light-up sneakers, almost battered beyond recognition. However, Taylor refused to trade them in for new ones. Lindsay made a mental note to take her son shopping on her next day off, and not give in to tantrums and pleas.

"Mrs. Phillips is a nice woman. Now, shoes!"

After two attempts, Taylor got the shoes on the right feet, and the Velcro fastened. He gave his grandmother a big kiss and ran out to the car after his mother. Once he was secured in the back of her forever reliable Toyota Corolla, they set out to face morning traffic.

***

Shaw crumpled his paper cup and aimed it for the nearest trash can. He had been working twelve hours straight with the death of Corrine Evans, consoling the family while waiting on his cell phone to ring and alert him to the completion of the autopsy. Although forensics had been in when Corrine arrived at the hospital—taking fingernail scrapings, waiting for the sexual assault kit to be completed, combing her hair for fibers—it was still standard protocol her body be examined for any missed clues. Even so, not even the results from the first round of evidence gathering had been completed. He doubted they would be in much of a rush to expedite the autopsy.

He rubbed his hand over his hair, groaning as the lack of sleep pressed on the backs of his eyes. In his fifteen years on the force, five with homicide, he'd become used to the long nights and painful days fueled by coffee consumption. The Evans case would be one of those which would haunt him forever. Corrine had been the only girl found alive, and as much as it would have pained him to hear the details, he hated the fact she hadn't recovered to tell them what had happened.

Walking out of the hospital staff room, Shaw stifled a yawn. He wondered if their killer would go underground now, not knowing whether Corrine had survived. He made a conscious decision not to release any details of her passing to the press, hoping to buy a little more time to process the evidence. While his thoughts were tangled up in procedure, he almost ran headfirst into Dr. Young.

She chuckled softly, bringing a hand to her chest. "We must stop running into each other like this, Detective."

His eyes brightened at her fresh-faced appearance.

"Yeah, it's becoming a habit." He turned, meandering down the corridor next to her.

"How's the family?" Concern flooded Lindsay's voice.

Shaw tucked his hands into his pockets. "Gone home not too long ago. Her mother wanted to stay until the coroner came, but they had a backlog. You just on shift?"

"Yup, another twelve-hour one for me. Shouldn't you be home in bed?" she scolded lightly.

He held up his hands, cracking a smile. "Going, going." They paused by the bank of elevators.

"You will let me know what happens, won't you?"

He could tell the question was hard for her to ask, but there were always those cases you wanted to follow through to the end. "Yeah, no probs, Linds. Take care." He gave her a wave as the elevator dinged. She smiled, and he watched her face vanish as the doors to the elevator closed.

Slumping against the wall, Shaw let out a low sigh. Dr. Lindsay Young had been a fixture in ICU as long as he could remember. She used to work in the ER, but had decided a few years previously that she wanted something more consistent than wondering what she would face from one night to the next. She was intelligent, gorgeous, and had a heart of gold. Shaw smiled to himself. In another time and place, he wouldn't hesitate asking her out for dinner or to a movie.

He thought about his wife, and their tense marriage. She would be back with the kids soon, and they would have to face the music about their relationship. It had run its natural course. She would be happier without him, and the looming dark cloud which came with his job.

The elevator doors whooshed open in the lobby, and the same, dour-faced attorney from the previous evening met him with a pointed stare. Shaw gave him a curt nod and brushed past him, moving out into the crisp morning air.

***

Edward barely gave the stocky detective a second glance as he stepped easily into the elevator and pressed his finger on the button for the floor corresponding to the ICU. The cubicle zipped smoothly upward and opened with a melodic ding. He stepped into the peaceful ward. Edward had timed his arrival well, knowing morning rounds would be finished, and most of the nurses and doctors would be in meetings.

He straightened the Windsor knot in his blue silk tie and approached the reception desk. Brittney had been replaced by a matronly woman, who did not look overly impressed at being disturbed. Edward repressed his urge to slap her pinched face and cleared his throat.

"May I help you, sir?" She crossed her arms over her ample bosom.

"I am here to see Frederick Jones. I am his attorney."

The woman eyed him up and down incredulously. "We usually stick to visiting hours for the ICU. Our patients need their rest."

Edward seeped honey into his voice. "I am truly sorry, Nurse..." He scanned her nametag. "...Bernice, but my client's father insists these documents be completed today."

Bernice frowned again. "All right, I'll show you to his room."

Edward spun on a heel. "No need. Brittney was kind enough to show me where to go last night." He barely heard her huff of indignation and cursing about the young nursing student's incompetence, as he strode down the ward. Rounding the corner, he stopped cold, watching as a female doctor exited Freddy Jones' room.

She cradled a few files in her left arm, scribbling notes into one with her free right hand. Her blonde hair was pulled back in a messy bun, some blonde strands breaking free. From this angle, she reminded him of a Botticelli painting he had seen once in the Staatliche Museum in Berlin. Portrait of a Young Woman, it had been called, featuring the profile of a noble woman in a red gown, waves of auburn hair accentuating her angular features. Edward resumed his path to Jones' room, once the doctor had moved on to the opposite room, but her image remained transfixed in his mind.

He rapped once on the door, pushing it open. "Mr. Jones?"

There was a new police officer stationed in the room. He stood, back to the wall, hands clasped in front of him. It was clear his predecessor had told him of the dealings the previous night, because he repeated the same procedure—checking the cuffs and departing the room, all without a word. Edward liked him immediately, even though they were on opposite sides of the law. No small talk, all business, just the way he preferred to keep his dealings.

"Mr. Jones, have you had sufficient time to think about your father's offer?" Edward stood at the foot of the hospital bed, seeing the papers still neatly stacked on the table.

Freddy chuckled, giving them a gentle shove in Edward's direction. "Yeah, but I think the old man's getting a bum deal. I signed them."

Edward stepped forward and scooped the documents up. "I will inform him directly."

"Mr. Haversham? Uh, I was wondering if I could see Pop. Ya know, let him know I'm sorry for causing him all this trouble." Freddy rubbed a hand over the back of his head.

"It can be arranged. I will organize your discharge and transfer from here to the private rehabilitation facility." Edward tapped the papers into a neat pile and slid them into his briefcase.

"And...the cops?"

Edward flicked his gaze over the almost-childlike man in the bed before him. His bravado drained, Freddy Jones knew he would be kept under close scrutiny from now on. "The judge will order your release this afternoon into the rehabilitation staff's custody."

"Thanks, Mr. Haversham."

Edward vacated the room, nodding once to the officer as he returned to his post. He retreated down the corridor to the elevator, pressing the button, and waiting for the doors to slide open. As he stepped into the cubicle and the doors began to shut, he heard an insistent voice. Much against his usual protocol, he slipped his briefcase into the narrow gap, and the doors swished back.

The female doctor from earlier tucked a strand of hair behind her ear and smiled with relief. "Thanks." She stepped in next to him and pressed the button for her required floor.

Edward felt a lump stick in his throat as his composure faltered. He let out a measured breath, remembering the control exercises he had learned as a child. "Quite all right, Doctor. You must be in an immense hurry."

She smiled at him, an expression which brought light to her eyes. "Us doctors always are. Never a dull moment in this hospital." She tilted her chin up, watching the illuminated numbers descend.

Edward tightened his hand around his briefcase handle—continuing the slow, even breathing, as he observed the line of her jaw tapering off to her neck. "I can certainly understand. My profession is often the same."

She glanced over her shoulder at his tailored suit and polished shoes, before meeting his eyes. "You're a lawyer, right? We do get a fair few in here." Her comment was factual, no malice detectable in her tone.

"Yes, I am." Out of habit, he slipped a hand into his breast pocket and withdrew a card, handing over the ivory rectangle. "Edward Haversham III. We mainly deal with wills and assets, however have been known to take on the odd criminal case from time to time."

Her fingers barely brushed his when she plucked the card from his grasp. "Plenty of need for that, I suppose."

The elevator halted, and the doors opened on her floor. She stepped out, turning back for a moment. "Dr. Lindsay Young. See you around, Mr. Haversham."

Before he could respond, the doors closed.

3

Edward crossed the concrete parking structure to the secluded spot where he had parked his Maserati Quattroporte GranSport. The car was an evident luxury, with full brown leather interior, and midnight blue exterior polished to a perfect shine. The V8 engine afforded him more power than he needed, and he knew anyone observing the vehicle might think he had something to prove. Quite the contrary, Edward was simply displaying his status in the greater community. He believed strongly each person was destined to be at a certain level amongst their peers; his was certainly higher than the average human being, including Freddy Jones.

He pressed the automatic locks and gently set his briefcase on the immaculate back seat, before sliding behind the wheel. The engine roared to life as he maneuvered out of the parking structure. The car had been a gift to himself upon making partner with the firm. The manual transmission—while unusual for the average American to drive—was a necessity, giving him complete control of the vehicle. Much like a woman, the slightest adjustment was all that was needed to make the Maserati purr.

As he drove down the busy city streets, his mind drifted to the blonde doctor. She was not his typical choice for female companionship. He had been introduced to a number of high-class women, bred to be sophisticated, elegant, and the ideal spouse for someone of his position and standing. Still, a doctor held many possibilities, and she had no ring on her finger.

Edward finally arrived at the glass office building. The valet was ready to take his car as soon as he drove into the secure underground parking. Retrieving his briefcase, he handed over the keys—albeit reluctantly—and allowed the man to return his car to his designated parking spot. He sauntered to the elevator, taking it up to the top floor office of Wilks and Haversham, Attorneys at Law.

At the receptionist desk, Zahra Hamid's fingers flew over the keyboard, inputting data, cross-referencing appointments, and any number of other tasks assigned to her by the firm's head partner, Bernard Wilks. Her golden-brown eyes briefly left the screen, giving him the slightest of nods, as she pushed her straight black hair to rest over the opposite shoulder.

"Mr. Wilks is in his office, Mr. Haversham. He requested you join him for lunch, as soon as you were back. Would you prefer your usual lunch choice?"

"Yes, Zahra, that would be lovely." He beamed at her, and she gave him her customary cold requisite smile in return. Edward knew any forced charm he possessed would be lost on the Arab beauty.

Walking to his office, located next to Wilks', Edward took in the view of the city from the floor-to-ceiling windows. He let out a low breath, before setting his briefcase on the polished cherry wood desk. After his lunch with Wilks, he would file the papers signed by Freddy Jones, and wipe himself clean of his association with the wormy man. He hoped he wouldn't be required to provide follow-up, but his father did pay for the best.

Pausing to straighten his tie and jacket, Edward departed his office, knocking politely on the door of his partner's.

"Come," came the customary response, and Edward entered, the faint strains of Chopin emanating from the Boise speakers discretely placed at either side of the bookshelf.

"Edward, my boy. How did it go at the hospital?"

Wilks grasped Edward's hand. For his age, he was still strong, due to working out with a personal trainer three times a week. His tailored Armani suits were cut to perfection, embellished with silk ties and gold cufflinks. Thanks to an occasional week on his yacht in the Bahamas, his ice blue eyes almost twinkled against his tanned skin. Capped off with dark hair streaked with gray, his entire persona exuded power and authority, as well as years of experience.

Edward returned the handshake, before taking a seat in one of the brown leather chairs after Wilks had returned to his own green leather one behind the desk. "Everything went as planned. Mr. Crawford should be pleased."

"I knew I could rely on your powers of persuasion. Seems a shame to waste all that money on such a delinquent." Wilks' eyes hardened.

Edward leaned back, comfortable in the presence of the elder man, despite the clear animosity Wilks had for their client. "I agree, however, what can we do, sir? It's simply a matter of business."

Wilks leaned forward. "Business, indeed. Personal feelings should not come into play. You are, of course, correct, Edward. Please, though, call me Bernard. We have known each other too long to continue with formalities."

Edward smiled. Wilks ritualistically repeated the same sentiments every time they spoke. However, it would not sway him from showing the senior partner the respect he deserved. "It's a matter of respect, Mr. Wilks," Edward echoed back.

Wilks laughed, a deep throaty sound. "Of course, of course. However, at this point, I must insist. We are partners in the firm now, and I do not want status to come into play anymore. Shall we adjourn to the boardroom? I believe Zahra will have set out our lunch by now." He stood, tucking an engraved silver cigar case into his pocket. He held out a hand, indicating for Edward to precede him out of the office.

Zahra had laid the boardroom table with a white cloth, stretched taunt. At two places near the head of the table, gold-rimmed china dishes, bordered with polished utensils, and each covered with a silver cloche sat, along with a bottle of red wine and crystal glasses. Wilks was never one to eat from takeout containers, 'like a heathen,' he had once been overheard saying.

Edward took his customary seat to the right of Wilks, waiting for him to lift his lid before commencing. He knew under the cover would be a perfectly cooked filet mignon, with a sampling of fresh vegetables and potatoes. It was a simple meal, but Edward did not believe in overelaborating his food.

Wilks, on the other hand, indulged in everything life had to offer. By contrast, he would have veal parmesan in rich red sauce with melted cheese and pasta. Edward often wondered how he managed to keep his svelte physique, even with a personal trainer, but he was not paid to ask such questions.

Pouring the wine, Wilks lifted his eyes for a moment. "When did the hospital agree to discharge Mr. Crawford's son?"

"I believe this afternoon, if we are lucky. I was unable to confirm with his attending physician. As soon as the papers are filed with the court, the charges will be dropped. The District Attorney was quite clear on that."

Wilks removed the cover from his plate. "Excellent work, Edward." He breathed in. "Ah, wonderful."

Edward took his cue and followed suit. It pleased him that Zahra was so thorough in her job. She knew exactly what was expected, and she always delivered. One day, when he was running the firm, as Wilks often promised, he would possibly offer her the chance to be more than just a personal secretary.

"Now, we have a few more things to take care of, once Mr. Crawford's son is released from police custody." Wilks' fork hovered over the melted mozzarella cheese.

Setting down the steak knife, Edward gave Wilks his full attention.

"Mr. Crawford has asked for a bit more security to his arrangement. The document you had his son sign was a test of fidelity. He would like a life insurance policy taken out on his son as well, to be paid out upon intentional or accidental death."

Edward's brow furrowed. It was an interesting, but not unheard of, request. Mr. Crawford obviously wanted to protect his investment in his son's future. "How much is he requesting?"

"Half a million dollars." Wilks resumed eating, ignoring the look of shock on Edward's features.

"I can't say I know of any company which would agree to this, not with Jones' high risk lifestyle."

Wilks smiles slowly, delicate wrinkles forming around his eyes. "Edward, have I taught you nothing? Where there is a will, there is a way, my boy."

***

Detective Gregory Shaw slammed his hand onto the flat surface of his scratched desk. "They *what?*" he shouted at the now-pale uniformed officer standing in front of him.

"Released, sir. By court order."

"You're telling me Freddy Jones shot at our boys and

is being *released*?" Shaw felt the heat rising on his neck. Even though he was homicide, the news had sent shock waves through the entire department. "There's something at work here, Reynolds, and I don't like it."

"Sorry, sir. Just relaying the news...the Cap is pissed." Officer Nick Reynolds shrugged his bony shoulders and turned to leave.

"Officer?"

Reynolds glanced back. "Yes, sir?"

"When?"

"This afternoon, sir. Hospital will be letting him out. The Cap has already had to recall the officer on site." Reynolds nodded and continued on, relaying the news as he went.

"Shit! Sonofabitch!" Shaw resisted the urge to throw his stapler across the squad room. He grabbed his worn leather jacket from the back of his chair, jamming his arms into the sleeves. He had to see this for himself.

After reaching the ICU unit at Lakeland, Shaw stepped from the elevator and stomped straight down the corridor. The sight greeting him made his hackles rise. Frederick Crawford aka Freddy Jones was being wheeled from the room by a fresh-faced private nurse, no doubt enlisted by his father. Dr. Young was watching carefully from the side, her face an emotionless mask. The suited man from before, the one who had been spying on the Evans family, was there as well, joined by another man, whom Shaw assumed to be Freddy's father.

Shaw's hands curled into fists at his sides, as he stepped back to let the victorious party pass. Freddy grinned at him, and it took all he had not to punch him in his smug, entitled face. He remained still, eyes fixed on Lindsay, who hadn't moved from her spot. She held her customary stack of files, her captivating green orbs staring at the darkened hospital room.

"Linds?" Shaw walked up to her.

"Detective." Dr. Young's expression softened. "I apologize. My mind was elsewhere. How are you?"

Shaw stuffed his hands into his pockets. "Pissed off, pardon the language."

She touched his arm compassionately. "Must be difficult to see a man go free, when he should be behind metal bars and concrete walls."

"Yeah," he grumbled. "Yeah." Shrugging off her sympathy, Shaw retreated down the corridor. He hated himself for being downright rude to Lindsay, but he needed to be alone.

Shaw went back to the parking structure. He was trying to dig the keys for his old Chevy pick-up out of his pocket, when someone tapped his shoulder.

"Detective Shaw, isn't it?"

He revolved slowly, taking in the face of the attorney. "Yeah, who's asking?"

"Edward Haversham III. My firm was enlisted by Mr. Jones' father."

Shaw lifted an eyebrow. "Charmed, I'm sure." The shadow of annoyance in Haversham's eyes didn't go unnoticed by the seasoned detective.

"Yes, well, I was wondering if you had had any luck in the case of that young girl who was murdered."

Haversham had his full attention. "What is it to you?"

"Call it, professional curiosity."

"Professional…wait, what kind of lawyer are you?"

"Wills and assets, but sometimes, we represent clients in criminal defense cases."

Shaw barked out a dry laugh. "Fishing for a case, Haversham? Well, you're outta luck. No leads. Even if I did have one, I wouldn't share it with the likes of you." He didn't allow the lawyer to respond and continued on his way to his truck.

***

He truly hated this aspect of his work. Hefting the body from the trunk of his car, he carefully slid it into the duck pond at the bank. On his way home, he would dispose of the gloves and tarp in a dumpster at the opposite end of the city. His plans were always foolproof. Still, he knew placing the body in such a public area may draw the attention of law enforcement sooner than he would like, but it didn't matter. He found the police to be highly incompetent in dealing with the true crimes of the city—his city.

Despite the warm weather, the coolness of the car soothed him as he turned the radio to a classical music station. Tonight, the composer didn't matter. He would soon have the city swaying to his flicking baton, bringing all the players in, one-by-one.

4

On his drive to the station, Shaw's cell phone rang. He pulled off the street and answered.

"Sorry to bug you, Detective, but we have a DB."

It was Reynolds again. Shaw briefly wondered if the rookie ever did anything else aside from relay messages. "Location?"

"The Duck Pond, by Baywood Park. Bunch of kids messing around found it."

"I'll be there in five." Shaw floored it, eventually pulling up alongside several squad cars and the crime lab van. He got out, moving through the trees along the bike path.

Reynolds was there, as predicted. He met Shaw at the edge of the crime scene tape. "Kids called it in about an hour ago. They thought it was a mannequin at first. Ya know, someone playing a prank."

Shaw zipped his coat, following Reynolds under the tape, but keeping to the set path made by the first officer on scene. One way in, one way out. Kept things clean for the crime lab techs, who were in white suits, scavenging the area.

The coroner knelt by the shore, the techs having cut away the trees covering the body. The body had been moved away from the water's edge, preventing any further contamination of the evidence. However, despite their best efforts, it was likely a good deal had already been washed away.

"How ya doin', Vic?"

Dr. Victor Espinoza lifted his head slightly in greeting, before going back to the task at hand. "Shaw. Welcome to the party."

"I know it's probably stupid to ask right now, but any idea what we're dealing with?"

Espinoza rocked back on his heels. "Too early to tell. Male, been in the water probably forty-eight hours at most, based on the marbling on his skin. Bloated, so an ID is going to be hard at this point. Once I get him on the slab, I'll know more."

Shaw nodded, addressing Reynolds. "Who was first responder?"

"Oh, me, sir. I was hanging around when the call came in."

"Great. Get anything from the kids?"

Reynolds pulled out a notepad. "Uh, teenagers, two boys and a girl. They're back at the station, waiting for their parents. Looks like they ditched school to…uh…do what teenagers do."

Shaw shook his head, looking back to the body. The face was swollen, and fluid leached from his nose and mouth. "I'll start with them. Vic, let me know when you have anything to tell me."

"No prob, Detective."

Shaw left the crime scene, Reynolds hot on his tail. It was clear the rookie was keen. "Stay here and be on alert."

"Yes, sir." Reynolds beamed with the opportunity to be involved in a murder investigation.

Enthusiasm—something which had faded in Shaw

over the grinding years on the force. "I'll be at the station, if there's any news." He crossed to where he had parked his pick-up, and got in. With a new case on the table, the Corrine Evans case would be placed on the back burner, so to speak. In all likelihood, it would go cold, unless new evidence surfaced. He couldn't bring himself to call the family just yet. First, he would deal with the matter of the teenagers and, no doubt, their really annoyed parents.

***

Edward stood back as Crawford embraced his son. The petite nurse wheeled Freddy, now back in the bosom of his family, to a ground floor bedroom in the expansive mansion owned by his business mogul father. Once they had departed, Crawford turned to Edward and shook his hand warmly. "Thank you for your firm's help in delivering my son to me. I can't tell you how much our family appreciates your role in convincing him to seek help."

Edward allowed the man to shake his hand for a moment, before extracting it from Crawford's grip. "You son made the decision for himself, Mr. Crawford. We were merely the middlemen in this arrangement."

"Yes, well, I would appreciate it if you could pass this on to your partner, Mr. Wilks." Crawford handed over a sealed manila envelope. "With my gratitude." He also slipped another document in his hand. "For Freddy's medical records."

Edward tucked away both in his briefcase. "Thank you, I will pass it on to Mr. Wilks as soon as I return to the office."

"Thank you again." Crawford escorted Edward to the door, clapping him on the shoulder. "I'll be in touch about the policy."

Returning to his Maserati, Edward aimed the car not for the office, but to the hospital. He had almost arrived, when his cell phone sounded. Answering it through the hands-free feature on his car, he spoke his usual greeting. "Edward Haversham."

"Edward, I am so glad I caught you," Wilks' dulcet tones filled the interior of the vehicle. "Did you finish the business with Crawford?"

"Yes, sir. I have an envelope to deliver to you, but I need to make a final stop at the hospital to gather Freddy Jones' medical records for the insurance documents."

"Good, good. Then, please return to the office. I'd like to wrap up this case before I go away next week."

Both said the requisite goodbyes, before Edward disconnected the call. He maneuvered the car into the hospital parking garage, leaving his briefcase locked securely in the trunk. He was the type of man to take the 'park at your own risk' signs quite seriously. Tucking the folded medical record release form inside his jacket, he commenced to reception, again facing another aging gatekeeper nurse who did not look pleased to see him.

"Basement level. Copying records has a $50.00 fee," she related to him in monotone, as if he wasn't the first person to come in that day with this particular request.

"Thank you, Nurse." Edward allowed himself to be cordial, despite the rising irritation at the seemingly endless slew of irate nurses and reception staff.

Stepping into the elevator, it was almost serendipity to see Dr. Young's face in the cubicle. "So, we meet again."

She peered up from the folder in her hand. "So we do. I'm surprised you remember me."

"I am very observant." He glanced at the lit buttons, discovering she was on the same path as he. "Records department?"

She bobbed her head once as the doors slid closed. "A couple of case notes to add to a patient's file."

Edward fell into the easy conversation as the elevator descended. "Don't you have orderlies to do that type of thing for you?" he asked, humor dripping into his tone.

To his utter pleasure and amazement, she genuinely smiled, the light coming into her eyes. "Yes, however, I like to see things through to the end. Besides, why bother an orderly when I have some time to kill. What about you?"

He patted his breast pocket. "Medical record request for my client."

"Don't you have paralegals for that type of work?" The corners of her lips twitched jovially.

Edward managed a smile of his own. She was quick on the uptake, and not short on humor. "I, too, like to see things through to the end."

The elevator doors swished open, and he stepped back, allowing Dr. Young to pass through first, before following. She revolved slowly, the question tumbling out. "Why were you with Freddy Jones when he was discharged?"

Edward placed his hands behind his back, studying her for any sign of anger or animosity. "I was completing a case."

Dr. Young wrapped her arms around the files. "You'll probably tell me it's confidential, but what is your connection to the family?"

Stepping closer than comfort probably warranted, he lowered his voice, "My firm arranged for the deal with the District Attorney and Mr. Jones. His father wanted his son to enter a treatment program." At this distance, Edward thought he caught a whiff of the doctor's citrus body wash, faint, but certainly there.

"I'm glad to hear he will get help for his drug problem before it kills him. However, I don't think the police officers he shot at will be too happy." Her brow wrinkled, as a frown formed on her lips.

Edward pondered her statement for a few moments. "We are masters of our professions. You, a doctor, must treat those under your care, to the best of your ability, without discrimination. I am much the same. Everyone must make their living in some way."

Her face returned to its former expression, relaxed. "You are right." She laughed, and shook her head. "It's been a strange day."

Without a further word, the pair progressed down the hall to the open-plan records office. Stacked behind a simple wooden desk, were rows upon rows of non-digitized files, dating back to who knew when. Edward stepped back, allowing Dr. Young to complete her business first. The young man at the desk greeted her warmly, almost as if she was the one ray of sunshine to reach the dank basement in years.

When she handed over the information for cataloging, he could see the boy's cheeks flush. Edward studied the interaction with mild amusement. Dr. Young certainly would have higher standards than this prepubescent looking youth.

Once she had concluded her business, amidst banal small talk, she turned to him. "Well, it was nice to see you again, Mr. Haversham."

It was a practiced expression, almost as easily said as breathing. Still, he made a leap of faith, much to his own surprise. "I do not make a habit of this, Dr. Young, but I was wondering if I might take you to dinner Friday night."

Genuine surprise registered on her face. "Oh…umm…"

The wheels were turning behind her green eyes. *What could she possibly be contemplating?* He was successful; it was clear from his attire and demeanor. Well-educated, well-spoken—there should be no doubt as to her answer.

"I am truly flattered, Mr. Haversham, however, I have a night shift on Friday evening."

"Another night, then?" He hated the pleading element to his tone, but his desire to see her out of this dreary hospital environment overwhelmed him to an uncertain degree. He caught sight of the smug expression on the file clerk's face, and anger knotted in his abdomen.

"I can't. Trust me, it's not because I wouldn't love to, but I have a great deal of obligations outside of work with my family." The words hesitantly tumbled out, and Edward knew her excuses were genuine. Still, it did not satisfy him, and he had the inkling she was hiding something more.

"I completely understand, Dr. Young. How could I be so foolish? Of course a woman such as yourself would already be involved with someone."

Dr. Young shook her head. "No, I'm not, but my family is the first priority in my life, only closely followed by my job."

"If you change your mind, you have my card," Edward smiled indulgently. She would capitulate in the end. All women did.

"Thank you, truly," she smiled back, leaving him with the file clerk as she departed.

The boy's self-righteous smirk faded immediately, as soon as Edward's stormy eyes met his. "Yes...uh...sir. What can I do for you?"

Edward withdrew the paperwork from his pocket, and slowly slid it across the desk. "Immediately, if you do not mind. I have little time to waste."

His Adam's apple visibly bobbed as he swallowed, and started typing. In twenty minutes, probably faster than an average request, he had the printer whirring to life, as it spat out sheet after sheet. He gathered them into a folder, and handed them across.

"I was told there would be a fee." Edward tapped the documents on the desk to align them.

"No fee," the boy stammered.

"Good." Edward gave the boy a crisp nod before leaving.

5

Dr. Espinoza was already snapping off his gloves by the time Detective Shaw arrived at the coroner's office the following morning. He pushed through the swinging doors, and met Shaw on the other side.

"Well?"

Espinoza sighed. "It's an odd case. We found no signs of drowning, initially, so I can conclude his body was most likely dumped in the duck pond."

"Any viable fingerprints?"

Shaking his head, Espinoza sighed. "His fingerprints have been burned off, teeth bashed out. His face is so contorted, we have incredibly little to go by, apart from a tattoo of a sword impaling a heart on his left bicep."

"Cause of death, if it wasn't drowning?"

"I need to run a few more tests. We found some puncture wounds on the arms and chest, with the flesh dissolved. On the forearm, some of the veins were collapsed. It's as if they were eaten away. The only thing I can possibly surmise is he was injected with hydrochloric acid, judging from the litmus paper test—it was dark red, indicating a high concentration of hydronium ions, which means absolutely nothing to you…" Espinoza smirked. "It's possible his fingerprints were removed the same way."

Shaw's eyes widened. "You can't be serious. What sort of sick bastard does that?"

"One who wants to inflict an immense amount of pain in a short period of time. There was some white residue inside the punctures as well. We'll send it to tox for analysis. My best guess is the victim was injected and then had the acid neutralized somehow." He shrugged. "But I'm just a coroner. That's your racket to figure out the whys and hows."

"Unfortunately." Shaw rubbed the back of his neck. Carol and the kids would be home that weekend; she had called shortly after he had left the teens in the hands of their suitably annoyed parents. "Can you forward me the tox report ASAP? I have some family stuff to take care of tonight, but I plan to look for an ID in the morning. DNA?"

"Of course. I took swabs and I'll forward them on to the crime lab as well. It'll be about 72 hours for results, since we had a rather sizable sample. They have a backlog as well, so don't hold your breath."

"Shit," Shaw groaned, "the Cap'll want this wrapped up quickly, before the media gets wind of it and blasts it on the six o'clock news. Another, 'Are our streets really safe?' double feature."

Espinoza tucked his hands into the pockets of his lab coat. "If you're lucky, it'll be kept under wraps for a while longer. Look, I better clean up in there. If I find anything else, I'll call you." He retreated back through the double doors.

"Shit," Shaw swore again. This really wasn't what he wanted to be doing. He'd much rather be poring through the evidence surrounding the Corrine Evans case than dealing with some twisted fuck killer.

Heading back out to his truck, he winced at the early

September heat, a stark contrast to the glacial air-conditioned coroner's office. Rolling down the window, Shaw sped off to the precinct. He hated the waiting game.

Reynolds was waiting at his desk when he walked in. The rookie was quickly becoming an unwelcome partner in his investigation. Bypassing him, Shaw went directly to the kitchenette and poured himself a cup of coffee, knowing the bitter taste would chase away some of the exhaustion pressing behind his eyes.

"Hey, Detective!" Reynolds followed him.

Shaw sighed, taking a sip from the mug before he turned to face the officer. "Yeah?"

"I found this. Thought I recognized the guy we pulled from the pond." He waved a newspaper article in front of the Detective. "William Holzer. Big time drug dealer."

Shaw squinted at the grainy black and white photo. "You got that from a bloated corpse? Either I'm losing my touch, or you're some sort of supercop."

Reynolds laughed like it was the best joke he'd ever heard. "Naw, sir. Just good at recognizing people, that's all."

Shaw wandered back to his desk, sitting heavily into the chair. "Can't make an ID off your gut, Reynolds. We'll wait on DNA. If it is Holzer, he's in the system."

"What about this, sir? The attorney defending him filed a missing person's report two weeks ago, when he didn't show up for a pretrial hearing."

"Uh huh. A lot of two-timing crooks skip bail, and a lot of two-timing attorneys file reports to cover their asses."

"I'm serious, sir." He handed Shaw another file. "He was reported missing by Bernard Wilks, some big shot defense attorney. He invested a lot into his client, it seems."

Shaw flipped open the folder, skimming the pages. "This guy's got a rap sheet as long as my arm. Why would Wilks want to deal with this scum?"

"Beats me, sir. Should I look into it?"

Placing the folder on the desk, Shaw looked up at Reynolds. "How long have you been on the force?"

"Two years, sir, nearly three. Been on the beat the whole time, but I'm due to sit my exams to be a detective."

He was eager, Shaw had to give him that. "Look, you can't just skip your other duties and assignments to play errand boy for Homicide."

"I know, sir. I…could you clear it with the Cap? I'd really like to start learnin' the ropes, ya know?"

Shaw pushed up from his desk with a mild groan. "Come on, Reynolds." Together, they crossed the linoleum floor to Captain Thomas Mancini's office. After knocking and hearing the abrupt grunt ordering them to come in, he swung the door open.

"Shaw. Better have some damned good news! The whole damn world seems to be riding my ass to get closure to the Evans case. And now this damn body in the pond. It'll have all the rights groups up in arms."

Mancini was in his mid-fifties, with gray hair and a matching moustache. He grabbed a nearby coffee mug and took a drink, making a face. "Cold. Damn stuff. Reynolds! Get me a fresh cup, would ya?"

The rookie jumped to, taking the mug and disappearing.

"Some kid, I tell ya. Spending all his free time here. Thought he'd be annoying at first. So, sit. What's the news?"

Shaw shook his head, lowering his frame into a chair. "You're not gonna like it, Cap. However, it's not why I came in. I know you hate no news."

"Damn straight."

"It's about Reynolds. I get he's only been on the force a couple years, but he's keen. I may regret this, but I'd like to take him on as a partner." Shaw related the thoughts he'd had earlier about Reynolds.

Mancini leaned back, lacing his fingers together over the slight paunch of his abdomen. "Partner? Dunno, Shaw. You haven't had a partner since…"

He lifted a hand. "I know, Cap."

"Right, let me clear it with his desk sergeant. I'll let you know in the morning. In the meantime, what's the Doc saying about our body?"

"Not much, until we get DNA and tox comes back on the substance found around some puncture wounds on his arms. Reynolds reckons it's some guy by the name of Holzer. His lawyer filed a missing person's report two weeks ago."

Mancini swayed side-to-side in his chair thoughtfully. "Hmm. Get on the horn to the lawyer, and see what he knows. No reason we can't make a couple inquiries while we wait for reports. Don't be pushy, though. We might need to come back to them, if it turns out the vic is Holzer."

Reynolds came back into the office, setting down the steaming mug.

"Reynolds, you're with Shaw until further notice. I'll clear it. And, for god's sake, get out of that damn uniform. Better hope you've got sterling reports, son."

The officer nearly jumped out of his skin with excitement. "Yes, sir! I mean, I do, sir. Been studying for my exams. I'm ready, sir!"

Mancini hid a chuckle with a grunt. "Get out of here, change, and go with Shaw. Shut up, watch, and learn."

Reynolds nearly tripped over his feet trying to get out of the office. Shaw raised an eyebrow, looking at Mancini, who shrugged.

"You did say he was keen."

Freddy Jones startled awake. He wasn't resting comfortably on his 1000 thread count Egyptian cotton sheets but sitting upright on a hard, wooden chair. He tried to rub his eyes, but his arms were firmly affixed to the armrests. *What the fuck had happened?* He tried to remember, but it was all a foggy mist.

Blinking, he looked around the barren room. His vision pulsated in and out as he managed to make out some metal locked cabinets, a table, and various white suits hanging along the wall. He couldn't see a door.

"Hello? Anyone there?" His throat ached, like it was coated in sandpaper. "Hello?"

The only response came from his own voice echoing off the wall.

6

When Edward arrived in the office the next morning, the insurance documents lay on the top of his desk. He picked them up, studying the squiggled signatures at the bottom with a frown. He supposed he should be grateful to Wilks for saving him another trip to see Freddy Jones, but he was unnaturally irritated at the intrusion into his case. He set the documents aside, placing his briefcase on the desk, and clicking the locks open.

His thoughts trickled back to the day before, and Dr. Young. She had played on his mind most of the night, and not even a rare glass of Scotch could lull his body into relaxation. Frustration and exhaustion, to Edward, were a deadly combination. Perhaps with Wilks off on his yacht, he would get an early finish, maybe take the whole afternoon off.

As he sat down in his leather chair, Zahra buzzed him on the intercom. "Sorry to bother you, Mr. Haversham, but there are two detectives here, looking for Mr. Wilks. Would you be willing to speak to them?" Her tone was clipped, and she clearly was annoyed at the early morning intrusion.

Edward internally groaned. Dealing with detectives

was not his ideal start to the day, especially since he had skipped his morning espresso. "Send them in, Zahra. Thank you."

He stood, straightening his suit jacket, and lifting his head as the detectives walked in. Immediately, Edward recognized the one from the hospital. He cleared his throat, putting on his best, dazzling smile. "Detectives." He shook each one's hand in turn, wondering if the younger one was even old enough to hold the title. Gesturing to the two chairs in front of his desk, he offered them a seat.

Both detectives took up the offer, the younger looking around at his surroundings, as if he wasn't used to the opulence of Edward's office.

"What can I do for you today?" He sat as well, leaning his elbows on the desk, and lacing his fingers together.

The older man fixed his blue eyes on Edward. "I'm Detective Shaw, and this is Officer Reynolds. We were actually looking for your boss, Bernard Wilks."

"Mr. Wilks is the senior partner in the firm," Edward corrected, watching the irritation flit over Detective Shaw's face. "He is currently unavailable, but I will be happy to help, in any way I can."

Shaw removed a photograph from his pocket. "We were wondering if you recognized this man." He slid it across the desk.

Edward retrieved it, peering into the face of William Holzer. From brief conversations with Wilks, he knew the man was on trial for possession with intent to sell, and solicitation of a minor. He set the photograph down again. "I'm afraid I cannot confirm or deny anything about this man."

"We know your boss reported Holzer missing, two weeks ago."

Edward's knuckles whitened slightly, as he curled his hand into a fist. *Impertinent detective.* "Mr. Wilks did not discuss such a report with me, Detective. Now, I am afraid there is no more I can tell you. My *partner* will return on Monday. You can return then to see what he knows." Edward stood, the customary sign to any visitor it was time to leave.

Detective Shaw did not take the hint, although his younger counterpart all-but leapt to his feet. He held out a hand. "What is your connection to Freddy Jones?"

"Attorney-client privilege. Now, if you don't mind…"

"And what's your interest in Corrine Evans, for the record?" Shaw's eyes narrowed, disdain on every feature.

Edward exhaled slowly. "I was simply a curious party." He circled the desk, opening the door, and calling out, "Zahra, please see these gentlemen out."

Without another word, the men departed, trailed by Zahra, who did not look at all empathetic to the situation she had placed Edward in. He shut the door, contemplating slamming his fist into it, but it was not worth the damage to the door, or his knuckles.

✳✳✳

"He's lying, right?" Reynolds quickly circled the truck, getting into the passenger seat.

Shaw couldn't dignify his question with an answer. Of course Haversham knew more than he was letting on, and it infuriated him. No doubt he knew all the ins and outs of the firm, what with Wilks away from the office.

"I know. He is lying," Reynolds admonished himself, without Shaw's help.

Shaw started the truck, steering the vehicle from the parking structure. "Why lie, though? What's he protecting?" The question was rhetorical, meant to help him decipher the possible motivations of lying about knowing Holzer. Reynolds, on the other hand, started yammering about what Haversham was hiding. Concentrating on the road, Shaw tuned him out.

"You hungry?" Shaw finally cut off Reynolds mid-tirade.

He patted his stomach. "Yeah, I could eat."

"There's a good diner not far from here. We'll grab a couple burgers and report back to the Cap. Not much else we can do." Shaw's iPhone rang, and he passed it to Reynolds, seeing the number was from the station. "Answer that, will ya?"

"Reynolds." Silence filled the cab of the truck as Reynolds bobbed his head. "Right, sir... Yes, I'll tell him." He hung up the phone, handing it back. "Seems Freddy Jones has gone off the grid."

Shaw tightened his grip on the steering wheel. "So, he didn't show up at rehab, like Daddy promised? I knew it was bull."

"That's the thing, though. His *daddy* reported him missing. Woke up yesterday morning, and Freddy had flown the coop sometime in the night. Real strange, I guess, too. Cap says no one heard anything, not even the security guard on duty. Nothing on their cameras either. Cap wants us to go question Crawford."

"Lunch'll have to wait." Shaw felt his stomach rumble, as he took the next on-ramp heading to the Crawford mansion.

After a condescending wave by the security guard, Shaw steered the truck along the paved drive, under a line of tall trees.

"Swish," Reynolds commented, leaning his head against the window for a better look.

Shaw kept his eyes fixed ahead, watching as the towering mansion emerged over the tree line. Standing outside the door, impeccably dressed, was Mr. Crawford himself, flanked by two burly bodyguards. He circled around the drive, and parked in front of the arched entry to the house.

"Detectives, I cannot thank you enough for coming so

promptly."

Shaw straightened his worn leather jacket. "I have to admit, sir, I'm a bit confused as to why you wanted us here. We're Homicide."

"Your Captain said as much, but it seems another client of my attorney has gone missing and turned up dead. I believe there is a connection."

Shaw exchanged a knowing glance with Reynolds. "Right, sir, we'll be happy to help."

"Let's go inside." Crawford ushered them in.

Taking in the pristine splendor of the Crawford mansion, Shaw was pleased to note Reynolds seemed to have gotten over his star struck mentality and was doing the same. They lingered for a few moments in the entryway, knowing the paintings hung on the walnut-paneled walls were no doubt authentic. Hoping they would get ample opportunity to explore the premises, Shaw directed Reynolds after Crawford with a nod.

The study spoke of a man with refined tastes, yet someone who had worked hard to gain standing, despite coming into wealth. Diplomas and degrees framed with pride, advertising Crawford's academic credentials, covered the walls. Above an elegant brick fireplace, there was a portrait of a woman in furs and diamonds.

"My late wife, Beatrice," Crawford commented off-hand, noting Shaw's attention to the painting.

He nodded, taking the seats offered by their host, who chose to sit behind the desk. Shaw was acutely aware of the bodyguards' presence on either side of the open study door. "You have a lovely home, Mr. Crawford."

Reynolds remained silent, but slipped a leather notepad out of his pocket. Shaw inwardly smiled. *The kid was learning fast.* He could focus on the questioning, knowing the rookie would be taking notes.

"Thank you, Detective. I do appreciate you coming. I hope it won't cause any issue at your precinct, my going over heads?"

"Nope, I wouldn't think so." Shaw crossed his legs, resting an ankle on the opposite knee. "Suppose we should get down to it. When was the last time you saw your son?"

"Last night at dinner. We were discussing his admission to the rehabilitation program."

"Did he seem upset? Agitated?"

Crawford rested his elbows in the desk, folding his hands. "Not that I observed."

"When did you notice he was missing?"

"My housekeeper, Tatyana, informed me, at breakfast, that his bed hadn't been slept in last night."

"We'll have to talk to Tatyana, if that's okay," Reynolds piped up, not out of context, and Shaw nodded in agreement. He was really getting the hang of this questioning business.

"Of course. My staff, house and security, are at your disposal."

"The Captain mentioned that there's no trace of him on any of your security cameras. Do you think your son had the skill to disable them? Maybe he decided your offer was too much for him to handle."

"Doubtful, Detective. Frederick was quite keen on the idea of the program. He wanted to turn his life around. I distinctly remember him mentioning how disappointed his mother would be in him, if he continued along this path."

"Beatrice?"

Shaw watched as a red color crept up from under Crawford's starched white collar. "Uh, no. Frederick was the result of an affair. My mistress was his mother."

"Was?"

"Believe it or not, Detective, 'arranged' marriages still happen in the higher echelons of society. My parents believed Beatrice to be a suitable match for our family standing, but there was no love between us—a healthy respect, perhaps. Frederick's mother was a woman I met on one of my business trips. She, unfortunately, passed away from cancer several years ago. I supported her, and Frederick, until her passing."

Shaw made a mental note, as he was sure Reynolds had made the physical one, to double check Freddy Jones' background once they were back at the station. "What was his mother's name?"

"Hannah Jones."

"So, your son went by his mother's last name?"

"Frederick didn't know I existed until his mother passed away, and he found I had been financially supporting her. He had balked at first, having thought his father dead, deciding he might be better off not ever having known me. When I found out about his latest troubles, I made one last ditch attempt to get him clean. I was so happy when he accepted this time. With Bernice dead, I finally could accept Frederick as my own and make up for lost years."

"How did your late wife die?"

"Heart attack last year."

Reynolds scribbled furiously on the pad, trying to get down every detail. Shaw wondered if he was drawing his own conclusions about the man sitting before them.

"How did you meet Bernard Wilks, your attorney?"

"Wilks has worked for my family for some time."

"Do you know him personally, or are all your interactions professional?"

"Strictly professional. Though, as of late, he has attended a few company functions, completely at my behest." Crawford flicked his gaze between the two detectives. "Is he under suspicion? I cannot see what involvement he might have in my son's disappearance."

Shaw gnawed thoughtfully on the inside of his lip. "I think we have enough to go on for now. One more question...where were you last night?"

The red returned from under his collar. "I..." He

cleared his throat. "I was with Tatyana."

Shaw tried not to laugh at the unmistakable ascent of Reynolds' eyebrows. "Then we will definitely need to talk to her."

"I would ask you keep this discreet, of course. I am not a philanderer, Detective." Crawford's jaw hardened.

"I would never presume, sir."

***

A man's love for his son was meant to be sacred. He knew this, if not from personal experience, but from the observations of those around him. There was no denying he had risen from the dirt, as they say, to the heights of society. Staring out his office window, this notion pleased him. Running a hand over the carefully combed lines of his hair, he wondered if his father would be proud of what he had accomplished.

He remembered the man vaguely. His father had been dedicated to his work, much like he was to his cleansing of the city. There was a morbid art form to it, and his hands tingled with anticipation at the prize awaiting him next. Playing with the previous victim's fingerprints had been intriguing, but he really didn't want to obliterate their identities. The world should know what lived amongst them.

His thoughts trickled back to the man restrained in his concealed room. Although he abhorred Jones, his father was even worse, placing conditions on his approval of his son. Perhaps he would appreciate him more once Jones was dead.

7

Lindsay rubbed her lower back, trying to dispel the ache building there, as the elevator descended to the lobby. It had been a long shift, with two casualty accidents and two admissions to Intensive Care on life support. There was a faint hope that, with time, they would recover, but it was looking grim. She hated days like this, when families sat at bedsides, clutching the hands of their loved ones, searching for a glimmer of consciousness amidst the beeping machines keeping them alive.

She desperately needed a glass of wine with trash TV, and to see Taylor's little face, relaxed in sleep, without a care in the world. One day, she promised herself, one day, she would be there for every school play, every PTA meeting, and every parent conference. All this hard work would eventually pay off, and she could be in charge of her own practice.

"Night, Dr. Young!" the cheery receptionist called out to her, as she exited the hospital.

Lifting her hand in response, Lindsay almost ran headlong into Edward Haversham. Flustered, she apologized profusely, before realizing who it was. "Oh, uh, hello again."

Haversham smiled disarmingly. "Dr. Young, I must be the one to apologize. I didn't mean to startle you."

She straightened her jacket and purse strap. "I was in my own little world. No need. Visiting a client?" She knew lawyers kept odd hours, but he wasn't who she was expecting to see at eleven at night.

"Yes, and no."

"Ambiguous answer," she quipped, wondering why a warming sensation was creeping over her skin as he smiled at her.

He laughed, shaking his head. "I only mean, I was thinking about our conversation before, when I asked to take you to dinner."

"And I declined, yes." She said it as a point of fact, not to rub in her rejection. She smiled, and softened her face to make sure he knew it as well.

"I was hoping you might reconsider. I have a sort of business proposition I would like to speak to you about. I'm thinking of investing in more philanthropic endeavors."

Lindsay shifted slightly, her curiosity getting the best of her. "Really? What sort of endeavors?"

"I want to fund a small charitable organization, working to help families who might not be able to afford medical care—mostly for children. I would be keen to have some of your professional input, if you would indulge me?"

She unintentionally crossed her arms. "This isn't some ploy to get me to go out with you, is it?"

Haversham held out his hands submissively. "Of course not, merely a professional discussion. For your time, though, I would like to treat you to dinner. Again, no strings."

Her mind quickly shuffled through all the pros and cons of the situation. In her profession, it was an asset to be able to swiftly assess any situation. She supposed there would be no harm in a discussion, although she thought it strange she had just been considering ways to spend more time with Taylor.

"I suppose I can agree to that," she acquiesced, watching shock, then joy cross his face.

"Excellent. When are you free?"

"My next day off work is a rare Friday night." She had planned to take some time to herself, as Taylor would be at a sleepover. It seemed, though, an apt time, and she wouldn't be worrying about her son meeting Haversham, and pelting either of them with an endless slew of questions.

"Seven? I can pick you up…"

"No, text me, and I'll meet you there."

Haversham's jaw twitched very subtly. "It's a small French place called *La Fantasie*."

Lindsay had to stop herself from gasping. "Are you sure? It's really expensive there." She remembered one of the nurses gushing about how her fiancé had arranged a table there to propose, and how pricey it had been.

"Of course, Dr. Young. I have the means. Please, allow me to treat you, while you listen to my ramblings."

She would have to dig out a dress—or buy a new one, her mother might insist on that. "I…"

"Please, Dr. Young. It would be my pleasure." His pleading eyes seemed rather practiced, but she eventually capitulated.

"Very well."

"I can't change your mind on picking you up?"

Lindsay ran through the scenarios. Taylor out of the picture, her mom had bridge with some friends…she could allow it. He seemed legit. "I suppose you can…"

"Excellent. Text me your address. You still have my card?"

"Yes, I do, but…"

Haversham smiled again, forgetting her request to meet

him there. "Perfect. I will see you Friday." He inclined his head, and turned to enter the hospital, leaving her slightly flabbergasted at the entire interaction.

She shook off the fog and made her way to her car. She'd have a hell of a time explaining all this to her mother.

***

"How well do you know this man, exactly?" Sandra asked, pouring her daughter a glass of wine. No matter how late Lindsay worked, she was always up waiting, unless it was an overnight shift.

"In passing, really. He's been around ICU for the past few days…with that guy, Freddy Jones…"

"He's missing. Did you hear?"

Lindsay's eyes darted open in shock. "Missing? I thought his father arranged some sort of cushy deal with the DA."

Sandra leaned against the kitchen island. "It was on the news earlier. Big press conference. That detective you know—Shaw?—he was on, too, requesting anyone with information on Freddy Jones to get in touch."

Lindsay shrugged. "I can't say I've seen him around the hospital, as if he would go back there. Seems pretty unlikely."

"Do you want me to cancel my night on Friday? In case you…"

Lindsay interrupted, "Mom, you rarely get out, what with all the help you give me with Taylor. Go, have fun. I'll be okay. I'll have my phone, so I can text you regularly, if you want."

Sandra shook her head with a smile. "No, you're a grown woman with a good head on your shoulders. I keep forgetting that, and see my teenage daughter on her first date instead."

She laughed softly. "I know you'll always look out for me, and Taylor."

"Lights of my life. Now, go give that boy a kiss and come back down. I've got *Project Runway* recorded. We can critique the outfits." Sandra scooped the glass out of her hand and took both into the living room, while Lindsay climbed the stairs.

The nightlight glow illuminated the face of her sleeping son, arms cuddled around three stuffed toys—Tigger, a monkey, and a blue bear. He never went to bed without them. She tucked the kicked off covers back up around him, and placed a kiss on his brow. He barely stirred. She crept back out, over the obstacle of toys, and pulled the door over. Her heart swelled. She loved that boy more than life itself.

Crossing the hall to her own room, she changed out of her work clothes into comfy pajama bottoms and an oversized shirt, before heading back down to join her mother.

***

Freddy Jones blinked, trying to shake the darkness from his eyes, only to realize he was blindfolded. He could hear someone walking around the room with purpose. "Hello? Who's there?"

A gag was stuffed between his teeth. He began to thrash, swearing profusely into the gag, until the needle entered his arm, and the profanities dissolved into muffled screams.

8

"Here it is, sir! Frederick Jones, born to Hannah Jones. I thought it was an alias." Reynolds handed over the birth certificate to Shaw.

"So did I," Shaw admitted, "but we had no reason to check this out further. As far as I was concerned, he was the court's problem. Things change though, huh?" He tried to ignore the hunger pangs. With the side trip to Crawford's, the press conference, and then back to the station, food had been forgotten.

"Look, go out and grab us some Chinese, or something, Reynolds. I'll keep up the work here, and report to the Captain. He did jump the gun a bit with the reporters, but I guess Crawford was insistent it go on the ten o'clock news." Shaw placed a hand on his gurgling gut.

"Right, yeah, I forgot about food." Reynolds hurried out, as Shaw's cell started to ring.

"Shaw," he answered. It was Carol. He tried to control his shock at hearing her voice. "Everything okay?"

"Yes, we…look, Greg, there's no easy way to say this, but the kids and I…we're staying out here."

"What?" He had to steady himself with a hand on his

desk. "You know, they're my kids too, Carol. You can't just take them out of state."

"I was hoping you'd see how it's better for them here. My family…"

He thought of his boys, trying to weigh what was best for them. "Summers, alternative Christmases. I want it drawn up by the court. I'll pay you support, whatever. That's my offer. You're free."

He could hear Carol breathing softly on the other end of the line, before she said, "Thank you. I'll…I'll pay for the divorce."

"No, equal split. You don't have to owe me a thing. I'll see a lawyer in the morning." He hung up the phone, sitting in stoic silence until Reynolds came back in with a brown paper bag. Suddenly, he didn't have much of an appetite.

"Sir?" The rookie peered at him curiously, as Shaw stared at the cell phone.

"I'll be back."

He stood from the desk and left the building, getting in his truck and driving aimlessly. It was late, but he hoped she would still be up, as he pulled up to Lindsay's mother's house. The light in the living room could be seen through the curtains, as he dragged his feet up the walkway and knocked on the door.

There was rustling from inside, and a chain latch sliding on the door. Lindsay opened it, her face a picture when she saw him on her doorstep. "Greg? Man, you look like hell. What's wrong?"

"She's not coming back. Staying in Montana with the kids. Sorry, I know it's late. I'll go. I…" He felt completely foolish.

"Come in." She opened the door wider. "Come on," she urged him, until he finally stepped over the threshold into the warm, welcoming home. "My mom's just gone up to bed, but I'm still buzzing a bit."

She led him into the living room, closing the door

quietly behind him. The TV was frozen on an odd picture of Tim Gunn, his facial expression warped. He almost chuckled.

"Sorry." She switched off the TV. "Sit."

Shaw slumped onto the couch, taking a moment to appreciate how Lindsay looked in her pjs, all casual and soft. He wanted to hug her, lose himself in her comforting embrace, but it wasn't the time or the place. "Thanks."

"What happened?"

"She called me, like, not even an hour ago. I agreed to a divorce. I'll get the kids for summers and every other Christmas, but who knows how long that'll last. They'll make friends over there and not want to come see their old man anymore." He was rambling, unaware of her placing a glass of red wine in his hand until he took a sip. It hit his empty stomach like a ton of bricks.

"I'm so sorry, Greg." Her hand came to rest on his arm. "Things were rough, though, huh?"

He nodded. "Yeah, not ideal, but still. To see something come to an end after so many years…it sucks."

"Understatement, but I get it. Still, you care about your kids. Taylor's dad…well, he was an asshole. You'll make the effort."

"Sometimes, I feel like I barely know them. I've always been working."

They remained silent for a few moments, before she asked the question he had been dreading to hear. "Why did you come to me?"

Shaw flushed, looking down. "I suppose, I only know other cops. I've got no family, and well, you always seemed to be understanding. I hope you don't mind."

"Of course not. It's kinda weird you know where I live."

He winced. "Sorry…shit. I'll go. I'm really sorry, Linds." He began to stand.

"Greg, sit down."

Obliging, he took on the air of a scolded puppy. "I may have looked it up, just in case. I wanted to make sure you and Taylor were safe after the incident with that violent patient."

Lindsay splashed a small amount of red wine into his empty glass, handing it back over to him. "Here. One more won't hurt, right?"

Shaw took it from her, their hands brushing. "Yeah, I guess I can handle it, if that's what the doctor orders." Before he could even raise it to his lips, his cell phone began ringing. "Damn, foiled again."

Lindsay shrugged helplessly, taking the glass as Shaw fished his phone out of his pocket. "Shaw."

"Hey, sir, uh, we have another body. In the pond."

"Another one?" Shaw was surprised to hear from Reynolds.

He sounded flustered, as if he didn't want to have disturbed him. "I'm sorry, sir. I wouldn't have called, except it's almost the same spot. In fact, the crime scene is still taped off."

"Unusual for the perp to do two body drops in the same place."

"We didn't think to station anyone there, sir, remember?"

Shaw inwardly groaned. "Yeah, I remember. I'll be there as soon as I can." He hung up the phone. "I'm sorry, again, for coming by unannounced, Linds."

She smiled warmly at him. "It's okay, Greg, really. Uh, are you free maybe tomorrow? We could get a cup of coffee, or something?"

For a brief moment, Shaw forgot the grisly case ahead of him, and felt his heart lighten. "I'd like that, Linds, I really would."

She walked him to the door, waiting in the illuminated frame as he got into his truck. He lifted a hand to wave, and she returned the gesture, as he drove off.

Shaw cursed his impulsiveness, but he couldn't have been more thrilled when she asked him to coffee. The feeling was enough to make him forget he had been drinking, although the one glass was hardly enough to inebriate him. He almost skipped to the crime scene tape as he arrived on scene, a very inappropriate reaction to the circumstances, but the prospect of seeing Lindsay the following day had lightened his dreary mood.

Reynolds hurried up to him. "Sir, this way. The coroner has just arrived."

The two men ducked under the tape, moving to the site of the body drop, just a few feet from the previous drop.

"Gentlemen," Dr. Espinoza glanced up from his kneeling position next to the body, "I believe you know the victim, Freddy Jones."

"Goddamn it," Shaw swore softly, staring down at the pale faced corpse. "We just left his father. Time of death?"

"About an hour ago, if the liver temp is right."

"An hour? Are you sure? Who found the body?"

"Would you believe it was the same kids who found the other one? Seems their parents' warnings didn't sink in." Reynolds glanced over his shoulder to the two teenagers standing with a uniform outside the tape. "Guess they wanted to show off." The boys caught the last part and hung their heads.

"Regardless, we have a fresh body, uncontaminated by water or any other environmental factors. Doc, how soon will we know COD?"

"Cause of death, I would guess, is this." He rotated the arm, displaying the dissolved flesh. "I won't know for certain until we examine it fully, but it does look similar to our previous vic."

"Goddamn it!" Shaw didn't bother to veil his frustration this time, earning a chorus of snickers from the teens. "Officer, take those boys home, and tell their parents what they've been up to. Again."

The snickers were replaced by protests, groans, and empty promises never to do it again, if the officer didn't tell their parents. They were unceremoniously ushered into the back of a squad car and driven off.

"What now, sir?" Reynolds shifted his eyes to the coroner, directing the collection and transport of the body.

"We go to Mr. Crawford and inform him we've found a body. He'll have to come down to the morgue and identify it as his son, officially."

✱✱✱

"Dr. Young, wait! There's a box here for you." The night receptionist stood, handing over the package to the bewildered Lindsay, as she was coming off her last shift before her day off.

She studied the immaculate white box with the purple bow. "Did you see who left it?"

"Standard delivery guy, Doc." The receptionist went back to her desk with a shrug.

She tucked the box under her arm, and continued on her trek to the parking garage. Once inside her car, curiosity overwhelmed her, and she tugged at the ribbon. It fell aside and she lifted the lid. On top of delicate tissue paper, there was a handwritten note:

I hope you do not find this too forward of me. I didn't want you worrying about attire for our dinner meeting. I will be taking you to Le Fantasie. Friday, 7 sharp. – E.H.

She tucked the note to the side and peeled back the tissue. "Holy crap."

She traced her finger over the stone-colored fabric of the dress, and over the crystal details at the cuffs. Checking the label, she didn't recognize the designer, Pamella Roland, but she was sure her mother would know. Suddenly eager to get home, Lindsay quickly replaced the box lid and pulled out of the garage.

9

Edward hummed to himself, overly pleased with the dress choice Zahra had made, based on his explicit instructions. He had allowed her carte blanche with his credit card, and hoped the good doctor would be delighted with the designer creation. Despite only having seen her in a lab coat and scrubs, he had no doubt the knee-length dress with the drop back would accentuate her concealed figure. Dr. Young didn't seem the type to let herself go. She was a busy woman, and would no doubt try to keep herself fit; he was quite certain of that.

He adjusted his tie in the mirror by the bookcase. Wilks was still on vacation, and Edward had agreed to take the appointment with Crawford on Wilks' behest. He had made it sound urgent, so he felt he best not put it off any longer, especially when he knew he had his engagement with Dr. Young the following evening.

A voice rose out of his desk intercom. "Mr. Crawford is here, Mr. Haversham."

"Thank you, Zahra. Will you please show him in and put on a pot of coffee?"

"Yes, sir."

Moments later, there was a brief knock on the door, before Zahra entered with Mr. Crawford. The old man's face was pale and drawn. Edward immediately crossed to him, holding out his hand. "Good afternoon, sir. I'm so sorry Mr. Wilks wasn't here to meet you himself."

"Yes, I understand." He glanced over his shoulder to Zahra's retreating back, waiting until she closed the door.

"Have a seat. Zahra is going to get us some coffee. What can I do for you? Your call was a bit vague."

Crawford marched with purpose to one of the leather chairs in front of Edward's desk. "I didn't want to say too much over the phone."

Resuming his seat, Edward reached for a pad and gold-plated pen. "I understand. Some clients feel more comfortable speaking in person."

The old man before him shifted uneasily. "Yes, well, how much has Wilks told you about my son? I know you finalized the last parts of the case, including the insurance documents."

Edward tapped the pen against his hand. "I did. Was there something wrong?"

"The police have been to my house. My son was found dead."

The pen ceased its movement. "Dead?"

"Yes, it seems he was injected with some substance. The police aren't telling me much at this point."

Edward's mind stalled. He recalled the officers who had paid him a visit the previous day about the missing client, Holzer. Two missing clients, two deaths. He grimaced subtly. Wilks would not be happy about this. He focused back on the task at hand.

"I am so sorry to hear that, Mr. Crawford."

"You see, I was really hoping to speak to Mr. Wilks. He had made certain arrangements with me. I didn't know he would be on vacation."

The door to the office opened swiftly, and the senior

partner stood framed in the opening. "Crawford, I am so sorry to hear the news. Zahra just told me." He crossed the room with authority, clasping the man's hand in his own.

Edward frowned, pushing himself to his feet. "I didn't expect you back until Monday."

"Circumstances had me cutting the trip short. Come on, Fred, we'll deal with this in my office."

Wilks glanced over his shoulder, shooting Edward a wink before they departed, leaving him in a state of confusion.

Zahra stepped back, as she was carrying a tray of hot coffee. Peering at Edward inquisitively, she shrugged, doing an about-face and following the older men. Edward lifted an eyebrow, slumping back into his chair with a slight feeling of irritation. He was desperate to know what Wilks and Crawford were hiding. Rubbing a hand over his smooth jaw, he contemplated the situation for a few tense moments, knowing he was wasting precious time.

Briskly crossing his office, Edward stuck his head out the door. "Zahra!"

She turned the corner, her hands now empty. "Yes?"

"I want strong coffee. Go to Starbucks."

"Starbucks?" She quirked her lips, giving him a slightly incredulous stare. "You hate Starbucks."

He leaned on the doorframe. "Do we pay you to tell me what I hate?"

Zahra raised her hands in submission. "Fine. I'll get my purse."

"No, now." He did his best to remain casual, as he handed her thirty dollars. "Get something for yourself."

Plucking the money from his hand, she cast him one final glance before leaving the office.

Edward stayed put until he heard the elevator ding. Then, with practiced speed, he hurried to Zahra's desk, pressing the red button which set the intercom live in Wilks' office.

The volume blared louder than he expected, and he quickly lowered it, before tilting his head down to listen.

"I can't shake this guilt, Bernard. He was my son."

"You have to trust me. This was for the best. How much was he draining you each month? I know you were funding his habits. Your daughter just had a boy, right? Put your efforts into him."

"I don't feel right about it."

"We'll funnel the life insurance money into a trust fund. I'll have Edward do the paperwork."

A panicked edge entered Crawford's tone, *"Does he know?"*

"No. I made that boy. I won't let him destroy this."

"What are you doing?" Zahra stood, hands on hips, in front of the desk.

Edward sat upright. "I was looking for the Tilden case. I must have flipped the switch." He got up, turning off the intercom. "Where's my coffee?"

"I remembered I had some letters to send for Mr. Wilks. I thought I'd do that now and save myself the trip later."

With a curt nod, Edward stood, moving back to his office. "Ah, yes, well, I'll get back to this file."

As he walked, a niggling feeling built in the back of his mind. *What wasn't he supposed to know? What could he possibly destroy?*

✱✱✱

"Mom?" Lindsay closed the door with her hip, careful not to drop the box.

"In here, hun! We're baking cookies."

Leaving the box and her bag on the couch, she entered the kitchen to an almost comical sight. Taylor was sitting on the counter, flour covering his hair, shirt, and face.

"What's all this? A ghost?" She kissed her son's floured nose.

"Cookies, Mom! I got to measure!"

Lindsay laughed. "I can see that. Why don't you go outside and shake off? Then get upstairs and attack your face with a washcloth." She helped him off the counter, dusting the excess flour off her hands.

"'Kay!" He unlocked the backdoor, running out onto the grass and wiggling his arms and legs.

Lindsay laughed at his antics, before turning to Sandra. "Something happened today."

Her mother set a tray of cookies into the oven, before placing the pot holders aside. "Well, don't keep me in suspense."

"I need to show you."

Sandra was clearly very curious as her eyebrows shot up. Taylor streaked past, stomping up the stairs, as they went into the living room, and Lindsay opened the box for her mother's inspection.

Shock crossed every feature. Sandra was an amateur fashion aficionado. She followed all the celebrities and designers in every magazine, and watched the award shows religiously. "Linds, do you know how much that dress is worth?" She fingered the fabric, running her hand almost lovingly over it.

"Mom, you know I have no idea about all this. I live in scrubs, remember?"

Gently extracting the dress from the box, Sandra laid it carefully across the back of the couch. "This is a Pamella Roland."

"Yes, that's what the label says." Lindsay dug her nails into her palm, wondering if she really did have a grasp on what she had agreed to with Haversham.

"About four-thousand dollars, give or take."

Struggling to inhale as her chest tightened, she could barely formulate a response.

"How did you say you met this man again?" Sandra inspected the crystals on the straps, admiring how they set twinkles shooting around the room, reflecting the light.

Lindsay finally managed to will air into her lungs. "He came to the hospital…to deal with a client."

"You never did say why he wanted to see you."

"He is interested in some charity work, aiding families who might not be able to afford medical insurance. He asked for my advice."

Sandra shot her a skeptical look. "Mmhmm, and does he buy all the people he meets with four-thousand-dollar dresses? Nuh uh. This man is after much more from you, not just your medical expertise."

Feeling heat creep into her cheeks, Lindsay groaned. "Mother…"

"So, is he good looking?" Sandra grinned.

"MOM!"

Waving her hands in the air, she went back into the kitchen as the oven timer started beeping.

Taylor bounded down the stairs at the same time, the front of his shirt soaking wet. "Cookies!"

Somehow, Lindsay lacked the energy to scold her son as she turned her attention back to the dress. She had two options. Return the dress, and tell him she wouldn't be tricked or bought, or wear it, go out with him and be treated like a queen, which she had no doubt he would. She had never owned anything that expensive, and the luxury of it twisted something inside her, making her yearn to feel feminine for one evening. It had been so long since someone had seen her as a woman.

Listening to the giggles from the kitchen, she lifted the prized dress gingerly, suddenly eager to try it on, and see if he really was as observant as he claimed to be.

10

Shaw flipped the pen back and forth methodically between his fingers. Crawford had displayed little emotion at the coroner's office. He knew from experience grief manifested in many forms, but there was something niggling at him. Crawford was too collected, too calm. In their short conversation, Shaw had learned he wasn't overly surprised by his son's death, assuming he had taken an overdose. Promises of remaining clean never usually lasted with hardened addicts, in his experience.

"Coffee?" Reynolds passed him a Starbucks cup.

The rookie was learning fast. "Thanks. So, what were your impressions of Crawford?"

"Cold." He sat on the edge of the desk. "Like, he *just* lost his son. I mean, I get trying to keep up appearances, but it was almost like…"

"He knew it was going to happen," Shaw finished.

"Yeah, that's it."

Shaw inhaled the scent of decent coffee. "It's probably too many years on the force. You get jaded."

"Naw, I saw it too. You're not imagining it, sir." Reynolds slurped his iced coffee confection.

Laughing, Shaw indicated to the cup. "Geez, man, you'll make the rest of us look bad."

"Hey, this shit's awesome. Could never drink it hot. You think we should check into Crawford's background?"

Shaw sighed. "I'd say yes, but that man's probably knee-deep in high-powered lawyers. I don't feel like opening that can of worms."

"So, what do we do in the meantime?"

Sipping the bitter, black coffee, he contemplated his answer. There really wasn't much to do. They had to wait on evidence being processed by the lab, and that could take up to three weeks, if they were lucky. Espinoza would be doing the autopsy, and that might garner something probative.

"It's a waiting game now, Reynolds. Either we'll get a viable lead from the evidence that brings us one step closer to our perp, or he kills again."

✳✳✳

The sleek, black limousine stopped in front of the Young household, the driver exiting the vehicle to hold open the back door for Edward to alight from the plush interior. He held a bouquet of white roses in his hand as he trod up the walkway. Ringing the doorbell, he felt giddy at the prospect of the evening with the lovely doctor, even if he had made up the very reason to get her to agree to see him outside of work.

The door opened, and he beheld the breathtaking sight before him with unabashed joy. Dr. Young was a vision in the dress, her creamy shoulders and neck bared in an alluring—yet modest—way, making her look even more desirable. His assumption she had been hiding something completely unexpected under her scrubs was pleasingly correct. Her blonde hair fell in elegant curls, framing her face. She wore minimal make-up, only to accent her already striking features.

Bowing his head, he presented her with the roses. "You look extravagant. I am overwhelmed."

For a woman with so much presence and control, Edward was surprised to see her blush at his attentions. "Thank you." She accepted the roses, smelling their fragrance. "But you shouldn't have." She indicated to the flowers and the dress.

"Yes, my dear, I did, and I will openly admit to being a bit forward. However, I live alone, and rarely do I have the opportunity to spoil a woman of your talent and beauty."

She set the flowers on an inside table, before gathering her purse and a light wrap. Stepping out the door, shock set in on her features. "A limo? I haven't been in one of those since prom."

Edward smiled, hoping to allay her fears. "It's customary to try to dazzle someone you're seeking to impress."

He could have sworn he saw her lips curve up, and her eyes brighten as he escorted her down to the waiting car, allowing her to slide across the cool leather seat, before getting in himself. The driver resumed his position, sliding the partition up to allow the passengers some privacy.

Dr. Young faced him, her eyes veiling accusation. "I have a feeling I've been misled as to the true nature of this little outing."

Edward held his hands up. "I am caught out. Yes, I may have fudged the truth slightly, but my intentions are purely honorable. You are intelligent, and someone I want to get to know, even if it means funneling money into a charity project."

Frown lines appeared between her eyebrows, her emotions warring behind the vibrant green orbs as she fixed them on him.

He didn't know why, but he was holding his breath. If she wanted him to fund a thousand hospitals, he wouldn't care. At that very moment, all he wanted to do was possess her. *Didn't he deserve the best?* Something shifted in his mind. Zahra would provide a pleasant distraction, once he broke her steely demeanor, but he wanted this woman on his arm at all events. His social standing would skyrocket, marrying a doctor.

"I suppose…well, this was pretty clever. And the dress is wonderful. My mother told me it was costly, probably too costly for a first…date."

Edward smiled, taking her hand up, and pressing his lips to the back of it. "My dear Dr. Young, you have made me extremely happy." He could overlook an overly-involved mother.

She blushed, the faint smattering of color visible only for a moment. "You should just call me Lindsay. Dr. Young is a bit formal, don't you think?"

He nodded eagerly in agreement. "Of course, Lindsay." The name slipped off his tongue effortlessly. "And you must use my given name as well."

The rest of the drive progressed in silence. She sipped the chilled glass of champagne he had pressed into her hand, enjoying how she didn't feel the need to flood the journey with mindless conversation. Dr. Young—Lindsay, he reminded himself—seemed to be a woman who would only speak when it was pertinent.

They arrived at the restaurant, the maître d' showing them in with great ceremony. Edward had booked the best table in the house, the Chef's Table. Although there would be noise from the kitchen, he was sure Lindsay would fully enjoy the experience. He could make a concession this once, to allow possible distractions.

As the chef cooked, providing them with delicate tasters, Edward realized the greatness of this decision. Lindsay sat next to him, a succulent scent wafting toward him from her neck. It wasn't any perfume he recognized from her time in the higher social circles. No, it was fresher, wholesome. Perhaps lemon, and maybe pomegranate.

Her smiles came easily with the chef and serving staff. Finally, they left them alone to eat, and he was bursting with questions.

"Tell me. What made you decide to become a doctor?"

Lindsay dabbed her mouth with a cloth napkin. "Do you want the standard 'I like helping people' answer, or the true reason?"

"The true reason, of course."

"I'm good at remembering details. Being methodical is a secret passion of mine."

Edward shifted his body toward her. "I take it most people want to hear the other reason?"

She nodded with a slight smile, which lifted her cheekbones ever so subtly. "Of course they do. Don't get me wrong, I like the helping aspect, but it's the logic of medicine which truly attracts me. Working to solve a problem, piecing together a puzzle. Isn't it the same with law?"

"I suppose so, although, it's not quite so black and white in some cases."

"Neither is medicine. I'm not heartless, you know. There are cases which still strike me to the core. Empathy is a big part of my profession."

"Yes, I could see that." They ate silently for a few more moments, before his curiosity overwhelmed him. "What about the man I was there to see?"

Her face clouded. "Freddy Jones is scum, if you pardon me for saying so. He shot at police officers, and that's just not acceptable."

"Was," the correction slipped off his tongue before he had a chance to check himself.

She stopped eating. "What do you mean?"

"I really shouldn't have said anything, Lindsay, but he was found murdered." Edward watched her face for reaction.

She inhaled deeply, offering no further comment on

the matter.

"I imagine there are some cases you cannot simply wipe from your memory."

Lindsay shook her head, the blonde waves falling back around her face as she ceased movement. "Children are hard to see suffering, especially if someone has put them in that position of suffering."

Disliking the doom and gloom direction of the conversation, Edward adjusted the topic. "Let's speak of something lighter. What do you do in your spare time?"

"My son takes up most of my spare time."

A son? That meant there must be another man. Edward inwardly scowled. So this was what she had meant by family obligations. "A son?"

She flushed. "Yes, Taylor. He's five. His father is completely out of the picture. My mother helps me raise him."

Edward rethought his earlier conclusions. Even with a child from another man, all Lindsay's accomplishments shone through. Who knew, he could even be lauded for taking on another man's leavings. The mother might pose some issue, but he was charming enough. He was troubled by these considerations, but he knew this woman was the one.

"I hope I get to meet him someday, if we continue our…relationship?"

Another genuine smile graced those full lips. "Yes, as long as you don't mind fitting in around my busy schedule."

"Likewise, my dear."

He swirled the Pierre Ferrand 1914 Vintage Millésime Cognac in the crystal snifter, watching the fire flicker through the pristine liquid. It was a mistake hunting so close to home. At first, it had been a matter of convenience, but now, it was imperative he remove himself from all familiarity. Throw the police for a loop. They were wiser than he gave them credit for—his first dangerous mistake.

Extending his legs out, he crossed them at the ankles. He had meticulously cleaned the chamber where Freddy Jones had been. It had been a challenge depositing the body in the same spot, without drawing the attention of any passersby, but a carefully aimed silenced shot to a dog walker's yipping Pomeranian had drawn the attention of any lingering public for just the ideal amount of time. It had been a planned distraction. The dog's owner was a waif of a woman, who had screamed and sobbed profusely. It had been quite the performance.

Running a hand over the supple leather arm of his chair, he considered his self-imposed mission—to rid the world of people he deemed unworthy of existence. Holzer had not been his first. He had practiced on the homeless, people the world would not initially miss and ones a coroner might attribute a needle mark on to overdose, rather than murder. As he saw it, he was granting them mercy, rather than having to live out their days on the streets. The promise of a hot meal and a bottle of beer was all it took to sway some of these undesirables to come along with him.

The first had been an elderly man. He had hesitated when he saw the military tattoo on his arm, but his mission was more important. The momentary lapse in concentration had almost resulted in failure, as a drop of the acid touched the skin of his intended victim. The scream was unexpected, but they were under a freeway overpass, and the roar of evening traffic dulled the sound. He had used too much that time, and the gaping hole was almost suspicious. A metal pipe provided the respite from the error, and he jammed it in the man's arm.

How clumsy he had been in the uncontrolled

environment, how frenzied, like an animal. He decided then, that that would not do. From then on, he would plan carefully for each victim, finally culminating with the first real kill. And there would be many more. In fact, he had the next ideal candidate already waiting in the wings.

Part II:

Cadenza

11

Lindsay leaned against the lockers in the staff changing room, flipping through the messages on her phone. It had been a week since her very memorable evening with Edward Haversham, and he hadn't failed to text her at least once a day to inquire how she was. She found his attentions overwhelming at first, but she admonished herself. It had been some time since a man had paid her any level of attention, so it was natural for her to be apprehensive at first.

Telling him about Taylor had not been a mistake, as she had worried it would be. She needed to be upfront about the number one 'man' in her life, and Edward had seemed to accept it with relative ease. She knew him meeting Taylor would be a big step, so she was determined to put it off until she was sure the relationship was going to work out.

She knew she was now the subject of the hospital rumor mill. After the mysterious package, two-dozen long-stemmed red roses had arrived at the front desk the day after their date. She knew now it was a date, but her irritation didn't linger. As her mother had put it, it was nice to be seen as a woman, instead of a title.

The screen lit up, as a response to her text came back. *In court today. See you tonight? E.H.*

Yes, finishing at 8. She tapped out on the keyboard, replacing the phone in her locker. Her break was almost over, and she had to check in with at least twenty patients on the ward before she could leave. Edward had all but insisted on seeing her, even if it meant a late movie showing. Lindsay had felt pressured at first, but she did want to see him again. There was something about him which tugged at her—a dark curiosity, a desire to solve what made him tick.

She pushed out of the locker room and headed back up to ICU, a smile on her face.

***

"It's as we initially suspected, Detective. The acid, when introduced to the body, caused the veins to fuse, blocking blood flow. The right injection caused a very painful death." Dr. Espinoza swiveled the magnifying camera to focus in on a spot on Jones' neck. "Here."

"Damn. As much as I hated Jones, that's not a nice way to go." Shaw studied the injection site. "Is this similar to the other victim?"

"Not just similar, Detective. It's *exactly* like the one on our other victim. I would say you have a serial killer on your hands, if I were to offer my own opinion."

Shaw let out a low breath. "I think you're right. Mancini's not gonna like this. He's prided himself on having a relatively clean city. Reporters are going to eat this up, especially since we didn't announce about Holzer."

Espinoza nodded. "You should go report in. Don't want this getting out of hand before you even have a chance to get ahead of this guy."

"Yeah, thanks, Doctor." Shaw walked out of the chilly autopsy suite, wandering down the hall in a mild daze.

"Detective."

His head snapped up. In front of him was Haversham, the smart-ass lawyer for the Crawford family.

He stopped in front of Shaw, a briefcase in one hand, cell phone in the other. "Do you know when the body will be ready for release? Mr. Crawford is eager to bury his son."

Shaw glowered. "It'll be released when our investigation is complete."

"Investigation?"

"Yes, *investigation*. It's a police matter now. I suggest you check with your client. Does he even know you're here?" Shaw brushed past Haversham, heading to the exit. He was in no mood to deal with anyone right now. One thing was on his mind, and that was to get to Mancini, and report.

Back at the station, he quickly located Mancini in his corner office, just about to take a sip of steaming coffee. When he saw Shaw, he set the mug down, eyebrows raised.

Shaw shut the door, before facing the desk. "It's as I suspected, sir. We have a serial."

Mancini groaned. "You're not serious, are you?"

"Dead serious, sir, if you'll pardon the pun. With Holzer's death, and now Jones', I can confirm the theory."

"Same MO, same dump site. I don't know how we missed Jones' killer dumping his body. I had ordered that area cordoned off and patrolled."

"The perp must've been watching, sir. Even patrols switch over."

"Yes, but it shouldn't've been unguarded for a second. We look damn sloppy. We should give a brief to the team, before Crawford starts riding our asses. You know he's in bed with the mayor." The mayor, Reginald Bridges, was a Republican, reliant on donations from some of the bigger business owners of the city. It was rumored he was planning on running for a Senate seat in the upcoming election, but nothing had yet been confirmed. To Shaw, he was as dirty as they came, but covered it up with all his charitable ventures. Mancini stood, placing his hands flat on the surface of his desk. "Damn."

"I'd like to get Crawford in for a more in-depth interview, if you don't mind. Something doesn't seem right. I'd also like to question that lawyer of his."

"Wilks?"

"No, Haversham, the other partner at the firm. Maybe both. It's strange both vics were clients there."

Mancini reluctantly nodded. "Sure, but don't rattle any cages. Like I said, I don't want the press getting wind of this bullshit. And do something with Reynolds, will ya? He's been prowling outside my office for hours now. Does the kid ever sleep?"

Shaw couldn't help chuckling. "Not that I've seen, sir."

"Well, report back to me when you know more. I'll call to arrange the interviews. We'll make it more a matter of protocol than the fact we might suspect something. Get your notes together. We'll hold a briefing tomorrow morning."

Shaw considered himself dismissed, and made his way back to his desk, unsurprised to see Reynolds circling.

"Reynolds, sit down, will ya? You're making me dizzy." Shaw rubbed his forehead and sat.

Reynolds quickly dragged a chair over. "Sorry, sir. What did Dr. Espinoza have to say?"

"The methods by which each vic was killed are the same. We're dealing with a serial."

"No shit?"

"We are going to get Haversham and Wilks in for interviews, as well as Crawford. Holzer has no known associates we can track down, so figuring out his last movements won't be easy. We'll start with the two lawyers, if we can get anything out of them. Saving that, we'll talk to Holzer's parole officer. One of the three is bound to know something."

***

Edward hummed jovially to himself as he left court. He had successfully argued the case for an elderly widow against her children. These bleeding-heart cases made him look favorable both in the eyes of his peers and the population at large. It made up for the times he had to defend the lowest scum of the planet. With pro bono work like this, balance was restored in the eyes of the community.

As he settled into the driver's seat of his car, his phone buzzed. *Caught on an emergency. Rain check? L*

Edward felt his back teeth meet and grind together. Plans being changed at the last moment grated on him, but he knew if he were to win Lindsay over, he had to be patient. If they did take their relationship to the hoped level, he would instill her in a practice of her own with set hours. Eventually, when they had children, she would stop working all together.

Sure. Hope everything is okay. E.H.

Tossing the phone aside, he gunned the engine. There was a melodic chime as his phone synced with the Bluetooth system in his car. Almost on cue, the phone rang. Edward pressed a button on the steering wheel, answering the call. "Haversham."

"Edward, my boy, excellent win today. Another gold star for the firm," Wilks' proud tones streamed through the Bowers & Wilkins surround sound system, filling the interior of the car.

"Thank you. It was a straight forward case. How did you find the client again?"

"Oh, a plea for help from a valuable source. Zahra will prepare a press release. We want this to shine, especially with the untimely news of Crawford's son."

Edward nodded, scanning the streets as he downshifted and pulled to a stop. "Any word from the police?"

"They want to interview us. Standard protocol, I am told, since our firm represented Crawford and had interactions with his son. Nothing to worry about, of course." Wilks had a habit of brushing over the important issues to get to the mundane. "The mayor's charity ball is in a few weeks. We have been given a special invitation."

Edward's thoughts jumped to Lindsay, bedecked in emeralds, her perfect figure encased in an elegant gown. "Might I bring a date?"

"Of course, my boy! You didn't tell me you were seeing anyone in particular."

I don't have to. "Yes, it's a relatively new acquaintance, but I believe she has great potential. She's a doctor at Lakeland."

"Ah, an educated woman. Admirable, Edward. I look forward to meeting her. I'll have the invitation placed on your desk. Have a good evening."

The stereo system beeped, before slipping into Tchaikovsky's waltz from *Swan Lake*. He envisioned sweeping Lindsay around the polished dance floor at the mayor's palatial mansion, her body moving in time with his. Edward smiled to himself, almost calling her that instant to invite her to the engagement, but he stilled his enthusiasm. There would be time enough for that once he got home and comfortable. After all, he didn't want to seem too eager.

12

Lindsay was finishing up her emergency case—a young boy who had fallen from his tree house in a daring attempt to emulate Superman. She rounded the corner and spotted Shaw. "Oh, shit!"

He shot her a bemused look at the outburst. "Well, can't say I haven't been greeted like that before." He held up two cups of non-hospital coffee. "If the mountain doesn't come to Mohammad…"

She smiled warmly at him, accepting the much-needed drink. "I'm so sorry. Things have been pretty hectic."

"You are forgiven. Things haven't exactly been a cakewalk for me either. We had another murder."

"Yeah, I heard. Freddy Jones, right?" Lindsay started to walk toward the elevator, but stopped as Shaw's mouth dropped open.

"How could you possibly know that?"

Shifting her pile of files and paperwork, she canted her head to the side, swallowing hard. "Oh, uh, Edward Haversham told me." She felt the color rise in her cheeks, an irritating reaction whenever she thought of Edward's charm from their date.

Shaw's face also reddened, but not from embarrassment. "What is that sleaze-ball lawyer doing around here?"

Lindsay balked at Shaw's reaction. "We...had dinner the other night. Not as if it's any of your business."

After a few regulated breaths, Shaw took on a very serious tone, the kind Lindsay had seen him use before when dealing with victims' families. "He's bad news, Linds. You...should steer clear."

"There's something you're not telling me," she probed.

"I...can't. It's an ongoing investigation. Just, please, be careful." His pleading tone cut her to the very core.

"He seems harmless enough. A little full of himself at times, but..."

"You haven't introduced him to your mom or Taylor yet, have you?"

"No, but..."

"I'm not one to ask people to do things. I mean, as far as I see it, we're responsible for our own lives, but this time, I'm asking. Don't see him, Linds, please. At least not until this investigation into Jones' death is over."

Battling between her desire to tell Shaw to shove it, and to tell him she wouldn't see Haversham, Lindsay gave the only answer she could think of to possibly placate them both. "I'll think about it. Okay?"

"I'd appreciate that." Shaw's brooding eyes returned. "Sorry again for catching you off-guard."

"It's cool, really. I'm just headed out. Wanna get a bite? I could use a burger or something." Lindsay was desperate to dissipate the tension between them. Her mind whirled with his words and a need to confront Edward about what Shaw had said.

"I gotta get back to the station, but I'll hold you to that invite another time." He gave her what he probably thought was a smile, but it came off more as a grimace. Lindsay knew his mind must be churning as well. She watched him stride off with purpose, her hands itching to get a hold of her cell phone and talk to Edward.

✳✳✳

"I don't know what you want, man. Come on, let me go. I can get you money…loads of money!"

He slapped the tape over his victim's mouth so hard, the man yelped in pain. He hummed *Swan Lake*. Tchaikovsky always made him feel lighter, forgetting his troubles as he worked, conducting his own invisible orchestra. He knew the police were finding bodies, and they found only what he wanted them to.

Closing his eyes, he swayed to the unheard crescendos of each measure. His first ballet was this very one. He had sat, captivated by the fluid movements. The dancers bent and twisted with practiced perfection. He knew at that moment, the finer things in life would always be within his grasp, and he would strive to keep them there.

The muffled grunts of his victim drew him from his reflections, irritation streaking over his features. He pulled on the gloves, measuring the acid into the glass syringe. He would take his time with this one. He had not been easy to track down, but he had succeeded where the police had failed. It was the least he could do for Corrine Evans.

13

Shaw's mind was on overdrive. What the hell was Haversham's interest in Lindsay Young? Did he know about their friendship? *Come on, Greg, get it together. What friendship? You have a passing acquaintance, at best. She's just being nice to you.* His fist nearly met the brick wall of the station, when Reynolds stopped him.

"Shit, sir, pardon the language, but it's not that bad. We'll get the asshole. Maybe you should go home for a bit? We're just waiting on forensics now."

As much as he wanted to hate Reynolds for saying so, he was right. However, he didn't want to go home. Carol still hadn't sent for her stuff, or the kids'. No doubt his in-laws would be providing all they needed and more. But he needed a shower and a change of clothes, at the very least.

"Yeah, I guess I should. Keep me posted. By the way, do you ever sleep?"

Reynolds grinned. "Nope, but I'll sleep when I'm dead."

"If only we were all so lucky," Shaw muttered, once out of earshot of his rookie partner. He made his way to his truck, dreading the moment he pulled up to the dark house, but it wasn't as bad as he thought it'd be. Mail was piled behind the door, and he scooped it up, plopping it in the wicker basket his wife had designated for that purpose. Wife? He had to stop thinking of Carol that way.

Going to the kitchen, he scrounged the nearly empty fridge for something to eat, reminding himself to go grocery shopping when he had a moment. Subsisting on fast food wasn't good for his health. He opened the freezer and found a couple of frozen lasagnas. As the plastic tray revolved in the microwave, he headed to the downstairs bathroom, blasting the shower. He'd taken to sleeping in the guest room, not wanting to occupy the bed he had once shared with his wife.

Leaning against the dark blue tile, Shaw felt like sobbing. The weight of everything going on was taking its toll on him. He hated the sit and wait game most of all. Either the trace evidence from the vics would come in, or they would have another body. Unfortunately, he was betting on the body.

Wrapping a towel around his waist, he padded back to the kitchen and retrieved his dinner, scooping it onto a plate and rummaging in the utensil drawer for a fork. Seeking any kind of distraction, he went into the living room and turned on the fifty-inch TV, settling back to watch the news.

The anchor, a bubbly brunette most likely picked to garner ratings, was rattling off the headlines. Shaw almost choked and paused the TV to catch his breath, rewinding a few seconds. Awesome thing, this TiVo. He increased the volume.

"In other news, Edward Haversham III, of the prestigious law firm of Wilks and Haversham, has successfully given Mrs. Felicity Grace Davidson a new lease on life."

The program panned to a scene outside the courthouse and an elderly lady in a black suit and pillbox hat. "When my Sam passed away, I never thought I would be fighting my own children to stay in my home. I am so grateful to Mr. Haversham for his help and support in defending me against my children's contesting of my husband's will. All I want is to live out the rest of my days in peace, and I hope my children will come to terms with what has happened here today."

Back to the anchor, who was all smiles and praises. "Wilks and Haversham often take on pro bono cases at the behest of their investors. They will be donating considerably to Mayor Bridges' charity of the month in support of the children in foster care in the Bay Area. This has been..."

Shaw tuned out, punching the pause button again. The same law firm who had represented the two dead men was being lauded as one of the most sterling in the community. This would put a serious kink in their case, especially since they had cozied up to the mayor. He stared at the congealing mass of cheese, noodles, and red sauce and his appetite fled as his cell phone started to belt out the Rolling Stones.

"Shaw."

"Sir, it's Reynolds."

"Yeah, I know. It comes up as you when you call a cell phone these days. What's up?"

He could hear Reynolds hesitate.

"Spit it out."

"There's another..."

Shaw groaned. "Don't fucking say it."

"A body, sir."

He looked up at the frozen TV image of the anchor. She looked comical, her face frozen mid-sentence, eyes squinting. "Right. Where?"

Reynolds audibly gulped. "This is bad, sir..."

"Look, stop trying to pussyfoot around my feelings. Tell me what the fuck is going on."

"The Evans' house, sir. It was left in their front yard."

***

Blue lights illuminated the houses of the quiet suburb as Shaw pulled up alongside the crime scene tape. Flashing his badge, he was quickly admitted to the scene, and met, on cue, by Reynolds.

"Fill me in."

Reynolds flipped open his trusty notebook. "Mr. Evans, that's Corrine Evans' step-father—I guess he adopted her? —got up to take out the trash around eleven. His wife confirms this, saying she had to remind him it was pick-up day tomorrow…well, today now."

"Yes, that was in the original case notes. Go on, man." Shaw wasn't in the mood for off-topic conversation. He wanted the facts, straight up.

"He said he saw something on the grass and thought someone had thrown their trash there. He got closer and could make out the face of a man. He ran in and called 911, then we showed up. That's about it."

"What time did the Evans go to bed?"

"Uh…I think Mrs. Evans said around ten? She was reading when she remembered."

"And she didn't hear a thing?"

"Nope, not a thing."

Shaw approached Espinoza. "Sorry to get you out of your bed, Doc."

"Eh, it's a living." He knelt next to the body with a groan, his knees audibly popping with the exertion.

Shaw hung back, so as not to contaminate any potential evidence. "Preliminary observation?"

"Male, can't say age yet, but he looks to be in his late thirties, if I were to take a guess. Overweight, beard, going gray. Wearing one of those suits you see on mechanics… Looks like there's a wallet." He carefully extracted the item to drop it into a waiting evidence bag.

"Hold tight. Any ID?"

Espinoza flipped open the wallet. "Uh, looks like his name was Dwayne Marshall. And look at that—I got his age right. Thirty-nine, forty in a month." He deposited it into the waiting bag. "The boys back at the lab take bets. Look like I've won the pot again."

Shaw ignored Espinoza's gambling habits, instead concentrating on the matter at hand. "Dwayne Marshall…are you sure?" He shone his flashlight into the face of the vic, and sure enough, it was the man they had interviewed months ago as a possible suspect in Corrine's murder.

"Yup, unless my eyesight is going in my old age." Espinoza creaked to his feet, arching his back.

Shaw glanced over to the front window, seeing the curtain drop back into place. "Suppose we talk to the family again, Reynolds?"

The rookie hovered near his elbow. "Yeah, sure, boss."

The pair made their way to the front door, knocking once before it was opened by Lorraine Evans. "Hello, Detective Shaw."

"Mrs. Evans. I'm sorry we have to intrude like this."

Her eyes were rimmed by dark circles, and he knew she would still be grieving for her daughter. He had intentionally skipped the funeral, but the force had sent a representative. At that moment, Shaw wished he had been more empathetic to the family's situation, but with his own problems, he couldn't have handled the grief.

"You have to do your job, Detective. Who is the poor man? Some homeless person?"

"Maybe we should go inside. Is your husband around?"

"He's in the living room with the other officer." She hugged the threadbare robe around her slim body as she led them through.

Jim Evans got to his feet. "Detectives." He nodded to both. "How can we help?"

Shaw gestured for the couple to sit. "We believe the body on your front lawn is that of Dwayne Marshall."

Both of their faces showed shock. "Are you sure?" Mr. Evans' brow creased. "He…no longer works for me. Left some months back after a dispute."

Shaw nodded slowly. "We are aware. I feel it might be pertinent to reveal we interviewed him in conjunction with Corrine's disappearance."

Mr. Evans took his wife's trembling hand in his. "I fired him before Corrine went missing. He was stealing from the company, and I couldn't see any way to forgive him. He tried to attack me on the way out, but some of the boys stopped him. I didn't know he was questioned."

"We made a thorough search through your employee records during the investigation, as a matter of protocol."

Evans drew in a slow breath. "I understand. You had to do what you had to do."

Shaw recalled how hard it had been to ask Evans about the death of his stepdaughter and his potential involvement. He was relieved when they had managed to clear him. Evans seemed like a good man, dedicated to his family. Still, sometimes the most unsuspecting people tended to be the guiltiest.

"Yes, we'll have a positive identification soon enough. I'm not sure at this point what I can tell you about the reason he was left here, but I'll keep you informed as much as possible."

"Thank you, Detective. We know you worked tirelessly to help us when Corrine was taken."

Shaw bit the inside of his cheek. Corrine Evans had only been one in a few cases of young girls found raped and beaten. She was the only one to have survived, even if it was for a short time. He wasn't going to reveal this to the Evans. The cases had been under investigation by the Detective Unit of the department. The city wasn't big enough to have separate divisions, like some of the larger cities. Reynolds was starting to look a bit green around the gills, so Shaw conveyed their goodbyes and took the rookie out for some fresh air.

"What's on your mind, son?" He guided him down the walkway, as the coroner helped hoist the body onto a gurney.

"Just…emotions, sir. I guess thinking about the family makes me queasy. It's hard to explain it. I can detach when I'm around bodies and stuff."

Shaw softened to the young man. "I know. It's a hard racket, but it's part of the job. It's that punch to the gut feeling, huh?"

"Yeah, just a bit. Is that bad?"

"No, just means you're human. Come on. Let's call it a night, and we'll get back in the saddle in the morning."

Reynolds smiled, putting his notebook away. "At the risk of sounding mushy, you're a good mentor, sir."

Shaw groaned, delivering a punch to the younger man's arm. "Shit, don't go all softy on me now, kid. Get some rest."

"You too, sir!" He bounded off to his car.

Easing himself into the seat of his truck, Shaw turned the key. There was no doubt. He wouldn't sleep tonight.

14

Edward grimly walked into the office the next day, knowing the detectives would be in around ten to speak to himself and his partner. He disregarded Zahra at the front desk and was glad she didn't try to force a conversation on him. Another positive trait—knowing when to keep her mouth shut.

He slammed his briefcase down on his desk as his cell phone rang. Anger was replaced with pleasure as he saw Lindsay's name. "Good morning, Doctor. This is a pleasant surprise."

Her amused laughter was pure music to him. "Yes, sorry. Are you okay to talk?"

"Yes, yes, of course. I'm just in the office. I had meant to call you last night, but I passed out on the couch." A little white lie. He wanted her to call him. All part of the chase—give your prey some room to wiggle.

"You must have been exhausted. I just dropped Taylor off at school, and I have the day off. Do you maybe want to get lunch? I don't know what your schedule is like…"

"Yes, that would be wonderful. I have something to ask you as well, so I look forward to seeing you. Why don't you come to the office?"

"Umm...yes, I could do that. I'll see you around noon."

After the customary goodbyes, Edward hung up the phone. He would introduce Lindsay to Wilks and get his approval before bringing up the charity event. Yes, this would work out perfectly. His good mood was quickly quashed by Zahra's voice booming from the inset intercom. "Detectives Shaw and Reynolds are here, sir. Mr. Wilks asks you to meet them in the meeting room."

He rubbed his temples. "Thank you, Zahra." After checking himself over in the mirror, Edward made his way down the carpeted hall to the room. At the table, as promised, were the detectives, the older one relaxed again, and the younger one poised with pen and notebook in hand, back straight.

"Gentlemen. How surprising to see you again." He sat opposite them. "What can I do for our boys in blue?"

"We'll wait for your boss, if that's okay." The older one, Shaw, yes, that was it, folded his hands on the table, staring Edward down. He hated it.

"Of course. Mr. Wilks should be arriving presently. Can I get you coffee?"

"Coffee'd be great, thanks," Shaw answered for the pair.

Silence fell over the trio like a smothering pillow. Edward kept his back straight, gaze direct, much as he had been instructed by his old law school mentor. Never let them see your fear, although he had little, if anything, to fear.

Zahra appeared with the coffee, setting white mugs before each detective as well as a bowl of sugar cubes and a small white jug containing cream. Her swift departure left a lingering scent of musky perfume in the air. The younger detective appeared vulnerable to her possible charms as he grinned at her like a schoolboy playing hooky. He blatantly ignored the hot coffee. The older one, Shaw, paid little notice, adding two lumps to his coffee and a swirl of cream.

Edward tapped his manicured fingers on the table, trying to avoid the irritation and impatience creeping into him. A waste of time. There was nothing he could tell these officers about anything they were investigating. As far as he was concerned, he had performed a service. It wasn't his fault Crawford's son was scum and involved himself with the wrong crowds. The old man never should have trusted his word.

"Ah, detectives, apologies." Wilks breezed into the room, holding out his hand to each of the men in turn. "You know how the law is. No rest for the wicked."

Edward watched the carefully scripted dialogue play out.

Wilks was all charisma and smiles, sitting next to him and taking up his own coffee. He let out a satisfied sigh as he sipped. "Divine. Nectar of the gods, wouldn't you agree? Some would be lost without this simple liquid."

"Yeah, I guess." Detective Shaw looked wholly unimpressed. "If you don't mind, we'd like to get to the point of the matter. You represented Frederick Crawford, father of one Freddy Jones, correct?"

"Indeed we did. Tragic affair. To be so happily reunited with your son, only to find yourself betrayed for an addictive substance."

"Mr. Wilks, I don't know if you're aware, but Freddy Jones appears to have been murdered."

Wilks waved his hand dismissively. "Of course, of course. What I only mean is surely he had fallen back into his old habits and someone took a dislike to him. It's not unimaginable, Detective."

"In this case, we believe Mr. Jones might have been the victim of a serial killer. If you'll recall, we did ask Mr. Haversham here about another client of yours, William Holzer."

Edward scowled. The disdain with which this detective spoke his name did not go unnoticed. He remembered him, poking around after Holzer's death, and from the hospital. Still, this tone was different, as if he wanted to take him out back and have a good, old-fashioned fist fight.

"Ah, yes, yes, Mr. Holzer. He was a client of ours. Are you saying you believe the same killer to be responsible for the deaths of Mr. Holzer and Mr. Jones? That is a stretch. The two men had very little in common, and ran in entirely different social circles."

"Yet, both were represented by yourself, Mr. Wilks, and your partner here."

The young one, Reynolds, reached into his pocket as the vibrations of a cell phone interrupted their conversation. "Uh, it's Espinoza."

"Take it outside," Shaw ordered, and the other detective left as he resumed questioning. "You also assisted in reporting both men missing. It's a pretty big coincidence."

Edward dug his nails into his palm. These assumptions would never fly in court. Detective Shaw was reaching, and he was half tempted to say so, but Wilks piped up.

"We have a stellar reputation, Detective. I can assure you, if there was anything untoward going on, we would never risk that for the sake of some petty criminal."

"And what about you, Mr. Haversham? Did you notice anything odd about the men?"

Edward narrowed his eyes. "No, not at all."

Reynolds returned and whispered something to Shaw, whose eyes widened. He nodded, and turned back to the two men. "Did you have any association with a Mr. Dwayne Marshall?"

"I cannot say I recall the particular name, but if you ask Ms. Hamid on the way out, I am sure she can confirm whether or not we received any communication from this man."

Shaw looked flustered, and Edward delighted in the thwarting of whatever vendetta this man had against their firm.

"If there is anything we can do to help further, please don't hesitate to ask. Now, if you will excuse me, I have some meetings to attend to." Wilks summarily dismissed the detectives with a breezy air and winning smile.

The gathered men stood in unison. Handshakes were cordially exchanged, and the detectives departed.

"Edward? Did you ever ask that lady friend of yours about the charity function?" Wilks inquired as soon as they were alone.

It was a very odd thing to ask after the police had informed them that two of their clients had been murdered by the same man, but Edward went with the flow. "She is coming to meet me for lunch today. I thought I could introduce you."

"Ah, lovely! I cannot wait to meet her." Wilks stared at the door for a moment before blinking, as if willing himself from some sort of trance. "Excellent. I will be in my office. I have decided to head home at lunch. I have some personal business to attend to." With that, he exited the room.

Edward frowned, sitting back down. He glanced over the cooling coffee cups and reflected back on the entire odd conversation. Wilks had been taking more and more time off, which was his right, he supposed, but picking up the slack was beginning to irritate Edward. He believed in everyone carrying their own weight. Something wasn't sitting right, and he decided it might be time to find out exactly what was ticking in Wilks' mind.

Lindsay approached the massive office building with some trepidation. The lunch invite had been on impulse, a subtle rebellion against Shaw's unsubstantiated request to not see

Edward. She had taken extra care with her appearance, for some unknown reason. She didn't consider herself one to be overly bothered with what she wore. However, today, she had French braided her hair, allowing the gentle wisps to frame her face. She had even applied a scant layer of make-up. The beaded, flowing blue tunic top and skinny jeans were borrowed from her mother's wardrobe, as well as the heeled sandals. It was an airy outfit, more than suitable for the warm weather.

She took the elevator to the designated floor, a whoosh of cool air hitting her as she stepped into the immaculate office. A woman behind a desk barely lifted her gaze. She was what Lindsay's mother might describe as exotically beautiful. Lindsay immediately found her pretentious.

"Excuse me, I'm meeting Edward...um, Mr. Haversham for lunch."

"Your name?" The woman took her in with glittering brown eyes.

Miffed by the abrupt and frigid reception, Lindsay opted to do what she always did when people judged her based on appearance—use her full title. "Dr. Lindsay Young."

The woman's immaculately groomed eyebrow arched, almost in surprise. "Sit over there. I will let him know you are here."

Lindsay, satisfied to have evoked a mild reaction from the woman, nodded and traipsed to a set of carefully arranged chairs opposite the desk. She made sure not to fidget. There would be no way that woman would get to see any nerves from her. The woman made a soft call on an intercom system.

Footsteps on the carpeted floor had her lifting her head a few moments later, as Edward emerged from a hallway, all bright smiles and shining eyes. She stood and he swiftly descended on her, brushing his lips against her cheek, murmuring, "Divine," out of earshot of the watching secretary.

Lindsay felt herself blush. "Thank you."

"I would like to introduce you to my partner, if you do not mind?" Edward encompassed her hand in his, and led her away before she could answer.

Edward rapped his knuckles against a closed office door, and opened it when the voice inside gave him permission. The room was awe-inspiring, with degrees, awards, and other commendations covering the walls. The man behind the desk reminded her of the suave charmers on her mother's soap operas.

"Ah, this must be the lovely doctor you were telling me about!" The man stood, extending his hand. "Bernard Wilks."

Lindsay took it, not at all surprised when he kissed the back of her hand. "Dr. Lindsay Young."

"Edward has said sterling things about you, my dear. I hope he is treating you well."

"We've only been on one date, but so far, he's been a perfect gentleman." She caught Edward's eye. He looked immensely pleased at the way the introduction was going. This was obviously very important to him, so she smiled at Mr. Wilks.

"Has he summed up the courage to ask you to our little charity ball in two weeks' time?"

Blinking, Lindsay cast her eyes up to Edward. A ruddy color was expanding over his neck and he cleared his throat. "I was hoping to…at lunch." She watched his masseter muscle contract in his jaw.

"Oh! I've stuck my foot in it, it seems. I am so very sorry. I shall say no more." Wilks smiled easily, as if it would defuse the entire situation.

Lindsay tucked her hand back into Edward's, giving it what she hoped was an encouraging squeeze. "I think we should get going. It was a pleasure meeting you, Mr. Wilks."

"Likewise, my dear."

There was something sinister to the man's eyes which had her stomach turning over, but she kept her face placid. Edward nodded to his boss and guided her from the room.

"Take the rest of the afternoon off, too, Edward!" Wilks' voice came from the office. "Treat your lady friend to a bit of fun."

"I will just be a moment. I need to get my briefcase."

Lindsay's stomach twisted again, but she smiled at Edward. "Go on. I'll wait by the elevator."

The woman at the desk's eyes passed over her again as she made her way over, but the odd exchange only lasted minutes, before Edward returned and offered her his arm.

"Shall we?"

Lindsay cast a final look back to the woman, who displayed two rows of white teeth in a smile which reminded her of a shark, as they entered the elevator.

15

Shaw did a double-take as he watched Lindsay walk into the building he and his partner had so recently vacated. He couldn't determine what was worse—his anger, or his disappointment. However, he reminded himself that she was not under his command. All he could do was try to advise her to the best of his abilities.

"Sir?"

Marching toward the underground parking garage, Shaw ignored Reynolds as his mind wrestled with the facts of this case. Three victims, two tied together by their use of Wilks and Haversham, Attorneys at Law. The third, a suspect in the murder of Corrine Evans. None of them were particularly good men, having potentially gotten away with more than one heinous act. The world was probably better off for not having them in it.

Reynolds wisely remained silent. Shaw smiled to himself. The rookie was coming along well.

"So, what do we have?" Shaw asked, as they both got into the truck.

Fumbling for his notepad, Reynolds flipped through the pages. Shaw managed to catch the pages of meticulous notes and diagrams. "First victim was Holzer, William. Parole officer says he was out maybe two weeks when he was found murdered. We don't know much about him aside from hearsay. Some say he was running a drug smuggling ring. He was arrested and charged with possession of an unlicensed firearm of all things. Released early for good behavior. His representation was...Wilks and Haversham, as we already know."

"Go on." Shaw drove on in the direction of the police station.

"Second victim was Jones, Frederick, known as Freddy. Son of business mogul Frederick Crawford. Mother Hannah Jones, deceased. Charged with robbery and attempted murder. Charges dropped based on a deal with his father to enter drug rehab. Found murdered not long after release. He had just signed a life insurance policy agreement with his father."

Shaw nodded. Hearing Reynolds relate the facts was much more helpful than going over them in his head. "And the last?"

"Marshall, Dwayne. He worked for Jim Evans, stepfather of Corrine Evans. He was a suspect in the kidnapping of Corrine. The girl was eventually found raped and beaten, and later died at the hospital."

Shaw shuddered. That case would forever haunt him. "What do we know about him so far?"

"Not much, aside from the fact he alibied up for the time of Corrine's disappearance. Dr. Espinoza called when we were in that interview, and said we could head over for his report. That's what I wanted to tell you, but I thought it best to stay quiet, sir."

Shaw both grumbled and grinned, making a U-turn at the next available spot and directing the truck to the coroner's office. "Coulda said so."

"I guess I should've, sir," Reynolds chuckled. "Anyway, Espinoza says he's got news about the Marshall's body."

"I'm dying to get into the bank details of Wilks and Haversham. Something isn't sitting right with me. They deal mainly in estates. Why the interest in criminal cases? It's peculiar. I want background checks on both by the end of the day."

Reynolds scrawled a note in his book. "Right, sir."

"Now, let's see what Espinoza has to say."

The coroner's office was as usual—the sickly smell of formaldehyde and other chemicals, and an overall permeation of death in the air. Shaw, despite his many years on the force, would never rid himself of the twist in his stomach at coming here. Reynolds, on the other hand, was appearing eager to get to the bottom of the latest victim.

"Morning, Doctor." Shaw crossed into the autopsy suite.

"Detective." Espinoza stared at Reynolds. "Still toting around the pup, I see?"

"He's growing into his bite. What can you tell us about Marshall?"

Espinoza lifted the arm of the victim. "It's as before. A puncture to the arm. Upon internal investigation, I found the veins eaten away. However, there was also a broken hyoid bone. It's as if your perp tortured and then strangled him. The act was done with precision, methodical. Not in any sort of rage. The vic also didn't struggle. He was either drugged or restrained. This is a whole new level."

"What do you mean?"

"Look at his wrists. No bruising. A man being burned with acid and then strangled would have struggled violently. I've sent his urine and blood off to tox. You'll know what was used, if there are any traces left."

Shaw sighed. "I'm tired of dead ends, Reynolds."

"We'll get the bastard, sir."

"I hope you're right…before he takes another vic."

***

He despised the seedy underbelly of the city, full of people ready and willing to take advantage of the weak. He considered women and children exempt from this. There was always a man involved, waiting to abuse for gain. He was an avenging angel—saving his Bay Area from the sins of the many people. And how better to find sin than let it come to you? The criminal population grew desperate when their neck was in the noose, so to speak.

The strains of Beethoven's *Moonlight Sonata* streamed from the speakers, and he tapped out the piano notes on the arm of his chair, contemplating the next victim. Perhaps it was also time to change up his *modus operandi*. No, the death by hydrochloric acid was just the right amount of horror and pain to inflict on someone who did not deserve the slightest modicum of pity.

He perused the front page of the paper. The police had already reported on the death of Dwayne Marshall, his body found outside the Evans' residence, as planned. How they could have been so naïve as to not realize the killer of a little girl had slipped from their grasp. Marshall had not been as dumb as he had appeared. He had not had a valid alibi for the evening of the sweet girl's disappearance, but it was amazing what drug money could afford—a willing witness.

Now, all he needed do was wait and hope the police would give closure to the family. Marshall was the killer; all that was left was a push in the right direction.

16

Edward's lunch with Lindsay was just what he required to take his mind off the unpleasantness from earlier in the day. They lingered over salami and pesto bruschetta at a local wine bar, allowing the expertly selected alcohol to complement their light conversation. Lindsay smiled and laughed easily, but Edward knew beneath the exterior was a cautious interior. They had, after all, only been on one formal date.

"Tell me about your family." Lindsay caught his eye, driving the conversation in a new, unexpected direction. "I mean, you know about mine."

Tapping his fingers on the red and white checked tablecloth, he contemplated how best to answer her question. "I grew up in a relatively standard home. I was an only child, both my parents working class, I suppose you would call it."

Her eyebrows shot up in surprise. "Working class? I didn't think…well, I assumed incorrectly. I thought you came from…money." Her cheeks pinkened. "Not as if that's any reason why I would, or wouldn't, be interested in you…"

Seeing her flustered made his heart thump with delight. He reached over and caressed the back of her hand. "No, Lindsay, I know what you mean. My name doesn't exactly inspire thoughts of someone who grew up with completely average parents."

She placed her free hand over his. "I'm so very glad you didn't take offense. To be honest, the interaction with your partner at the firm did frazzle me slightly. What charity ball was Mr. Wilks talking about?"

Grateful for the shift away from his childhood, Edward smiled, his earlier annoyance slipping away. "Ah, yes, of course. I am quite disappointed he spoiled my surprise, but nonetheless. The mayor is hosting a charity function of sorts, a masquerade ball, in two weeks, a sort of token nod to Halloween, as it were, and I would like you to accompany me as my date, if you're willing." He left his hand cradled between hers, enjoying her soft touch.

"I…would have to know a specific date, of course, but I am due some vacation time, so as long as it's okay with my mother, I don't see why not."

"Excellent. Would you allow me to provide you with another gown? I know the first time seemed extravagant, but I want you to feel completely at ease."

"I…"

"Please. Allow me this pleasure, Lindsay. The vision of you in the dress from our date has hardly left my mind." Edward spoke the truth. She had haunted his waking moments, and nightly dreams.

She pursed her lips, letting out a long breath, before her lips curved upward. "Sure! Why not?" She lifted her wine glass, and he marked the trembling in her hands. Was it possible he was unnerving her? Or was she starting to warm further to him? The prospect delighted him.

"You were telling me about your family?"

Damn! "Ah, yes, well, unfortunately, my parents died in a car accident when I was ten. I went to live with my maternal grandmother. She was not a woman of means, either, but still managed to send me to the best schools, although I did get through on a few scholarships. I graduated from Harvard with high honors, passed the bar examination, and here I am today. I still do not know how she managed, but I was grateful for her kindness after the death of my parents. She passed away five years ago."

"Oh, I'm so sorry."

"No need to be. Such is the way of humanity. We live, and we die."

Understanding entered her gentle gaze. "Yes, this is certainly how I look at things. However, it's sometimes harder to accept when faced with the reality of it."

"You are absolutely correct." He flashed the Cartier watch on his wrist, an overly expensive gift from a client, but wholly practical for a man of his position, and certainly not as cliché as a Rolex. "Well, since Mr. Wilks has given me the afternoon off, what would you like to do now?"

"You did mention something about a dress."

Edward inwardly grimaced, but then reconsidered. Most women loved shopping, and he got the impression Lindsay was not one who might often spoil herself. If he could cater to her needs in such an unexpected way, she would warm to him all the faster, and he would reach his goal all the sooner.

"You want to go shopping now? Before you check with your mother?" he teased lightly, running a thumb over the back of her hand, and curving his fingers around it.

"I…think she will approve. However, this time, I do think you'll have to meet her…and Taylor."

The guard was dropping. "It would be my honor and privilege. Let me make a few calls."

Mancini scowled at Shaw and Reynolds. "This is cutting it too close. The commissioner is riding my ass for a progress report. He also wants to know why the hell a man we initially suspected in the Corrine Evans abduction ended up dead on her parents' front lawn!"

Shaw leaned against a filing cabinet. "Does he want us to also magically pull the real Jack the Ripper out of our asses too?"

"This is serious, Shaw. Your ass, my ass, *his* ass are all on the line. The mayor's little charity thing is going to happen next week, and the fact we still have a killer on the loose in his city is starting to cause friction."

"What more can we do, Cap? Espinoza's found nothing on the bodies, aside from the injection sites and the acid. We've questioned all the witnesses, including those two pricks at the law firm. Nothing."

"What about Dr. Lindsay Young? You said you saw her entering the building."

Shaw directed his steely eyes on Reynolds, who visibly shrank in the chair.

"I had to include it, sir."

"All well and good going behind your superior's back," Shaw muttered. "Yeah, we'll talk to her."

"Good! Maybe she'll have some insight to this Haversham. Get out of my office."

Shaw spun on Reynolds as soon as they were clear of the Captain's hearing. "You *never* report anything unless you run it by me, got it?"

"Sorry, sir, I…"

"No excuses. Just don't fucking do it again," he growled through clenched teeth. "Come on. Dr. Young will be on shift, I'm betting. Call the hospital. If not, we'll go to her house."

***

Shaw was unexpectedly irritated at the nurse on the front desk who informed him Dr. Young had the day off. Likewise, they had little luck at her home. He was about to pull away from the curb when a Maserati came speeding up. Lindsay got out of the passenger side, but not before leaning over and giving the driver a kiss on the cheek. She carried several large bags, as well as a garment one. On a second glance, Shaw gritted his teeth as he caught sight of the driver.

"That's Haversham, isn't it?" Reynolds stated the obvious. He whistled low. "That's some car. Damn. He must be minted."

Shaw remained silent, waiting for the car to pull away, and Lindsay to go inside. Neither had seen his truck parked across the street.

"Should we go talk to her now?" Reynolds reached for the door handle.

Weighing his options, Shaw nixed coming back on his own later. It wouldn't be wise, and he had the feeling she was already avoiding him after he told her not to see Haversham. Gut feelings in his line of work were a trick of the trade. Seasoned detectives didn't ignore when something felt wrong.

"Yeah, let's go. Hey, why don't you take the lead on this one? Consider it on-the-job training." Shaw didn't trust himself to be rational.

"Really? You think I'm ready for that?" Reynolds' voice unintentionally squeaked.

"Sure, why not? Besides, best way to learn to swim is dive in feet first."

"As long as there's a lifeguard to save me from drowning if I fuck up."

Shaw opened the door to the truck. *Yeah, but who would save the lifeguard?*

17

Lindsay had just placed the garment bag on the back of the couch, when there was a knock at the door. She laughed to herself, pulling it open. "Couldn't wait until next week, Ed…" She trailed off, surprised to see Shaw and another man standing there. "Oh. Detective Shaw."

"Dr. Young. This is my partner, Officer Reynolds." The younger man smiled and nodded. "Can we come in and ask you a few questions?"

Dumbfounded, Lindsay opened the door wider. "Sure, come on in." She gestured toward the living room, where both men followed. "Coffee?"

"Uh, no thanks. Reynolds?"

"I'm good, sir."

Both sat in unison on the couch. Perching on the edge of an armchair, Lindsay looked to Shaw, but flicked her head back when Reynolds spoke. "We wanted to inquire more about your acquaintance with a man called Edward Haversham."

Lindsay felt the color rise in her cheeks, her neck heating up. "Oh?" She stared back to Shaw, who avoided her gaze pointedly. "What about him?"

"We…became aware you spent the afternoon with him." Reynolds hesitated before adding, "We have some suspicions he and his boss…"

"Partner," Lindsay corrected.

"Ah, yes, partner may have some knowledge about a few missing persons cases we are currently investigating."

"I thought you were homicide." Her question was aimed at Shaw, who continued to look decidedly uncomfortable.

"Yes…umm…subsequently, those persons have turned up murdered."

Lindsay's face hardened. "What is it, exactly, you are asking me?"

Reynolds cleared his throat. "Due to your…acquaintance with Mr. Haversham, we wanted to inquire if you…had heard anything about either a William Holzer, Freddy Jones, or Dwayne Marshall in your time spent with Mr. Haversham."

The younger officer was growing more uncomfortable by the minute with his line of questioning. Lindsay wondered why Shaw had let him take the lead.

"How did you find out I was spending time with Mr. Haversham?"

"We had just left the building and saw you enter. Unless you're looking for an attorney for wills and estates, we only assumed you were meeting someone. Then, as we pulled up to your home to question you about it, we saw you…getting out of his car." Shaw finally spoke up, his concerned eyes meeting hers. He'd evidently not told his younger partner about his earlier warning to her.

"Am I under suspicion of anything?"

Reynolds shifted his eyes between the pair. "Actually…I'll have that coffee. Is it…?" He gestured to the archway leading to the kitchen.

Lindsay kept her attention fixed on Shaw. "Sure, help yourself."

Stumbling to his feet, Reynolds moved like he was running from an escaped lion. "Thanks, ma'am."

Shaw remained unnervingly silent.

"What the hell is going on, Greg?"

He lowered his voice to a husky whisper, "I told you to stay away, Linds." He shot a hesitant look over his shoulder. "Haversham and Wilks were the last ones to see our first two vics alive."

"And the third?"

"We've yet to link him to anyone, but I have my suspicions. I told you they were bad news. I couldn't bear it if…"

Reynolds came back into the room carrying a mug of coffee. Lindsay shot back in her seat. "I, uh, see, Detective Shaw. Thank you for your concern."

Shaw motioned to Reynolds. "I'll have one of those."

The poor boy shifted, making the wise decision to retreat to the kitchen once more.

"What I do in my personal life is my decision, Greg! I told you that before." Lindsay's green eyes pierced into the detective. She was not at all amused by his meddling in her affairs, even if her own niggling concerns had been pushed down.

"I've known you a while, and I know when you're worried. Your eyebrows draw together and that…hard look comes into your eyes. Damn it, Linds, I care about you." The last bit came out in a rushed hiss.

She let out a low breath, trying to stop her heart from hammering. "I wish I could help you, Greg, I really do, but all I can promise is to keep my eyes, and ears, open. I do like Edward, but you're right about those feelings, for lack of a better word. He's invited me to the mayor's charity function. It could be a great opportunity for me to make some connections and maybe stop working these damned hospital shifts."

Reynolds returned with a second mug, still carrying his

own.

"Sorry, could you make me one as well?" Lindsay plastered on her most sincere smile, as her stomach churned.

Forlorn, the officer set down one mug, and returned to the kitchen.

Shaw shook his head. "Poor kid. He's probably confused as all hell right now. I told him he'd take the lead." He picked up the mug. "I don't want to tell you how to lead your life, but if anything happens, *anything* you think might be related to the case, I need you to tell me. I don't like sending a civilian in, and the Cap would have my ass for breakfast if he knew I was asking this, but I need your help. My gut is telling me he's the one, but be careful."

Standing, he went to the door, possibly forgetting about his partner in the kitchen. Reynolds came back through just as Lindsay was about to open it for him. "Uh…"

"Thank you for the coffee." Lindsay took the mug from him graciously. "But Detective Shaw seems to have been reminded of something he needs to do." She watched the pair depart, trying not to laugh at the poor, befuddled Reynolds. Closing the door behind them, she leaned against it, catching sight of the garment bag still draped over the back of a chair.

Setting down her mug on the side table, she headed toward it, drawing down the zipper. The midnight blue, strapless, floor length Alexander McQueen gown appeared, and she ran a finger over the satiny fabric. It was a near-replica of the one Sandra Bullock had worn at the Academy Awards in 2014. The price tag had been outlandish, but once she had put it on and modeled it for Edward, he was positive she would appear at his side. He said her blonde hair made her look like a goddess in it. She had allowed her heart to flutter girlishly at his words.

Returning the dress to the bag, she hoisted the

purchases, carrying them upstairs. As she hung everything up, she heard the front door burst open and Taylor's loud shouts as he stomped in, followed by her mother. Lindsay bit her lip, Greg's words echoing in her head. She had a family to protect, and if Edward would threaten that, it wasn't worth any possible accolades she could gain by her association with him. Wiping the worry lines from her face, she headed back downstairs for a much-needed hug from her little boy.

✱✱✱

Shaw made his way into Mancini's office, opening the door after a brief knock. "Sir, I have a request."

Mancini lifted his head from the pile of paperwork before him and removed his reading glasses, a silent indication for Shaw to elaborate.

"We're running extra security for the mayor's ball, correct?"

"We are, however…"

"I want to be on the detail, sir. I have a feeling I can't explain, but I know something is going to happen there." Shaw was adamant, leaning forward on his superior's desk.

Mancini leaned back in his chair, silently considering the request. Shaw fidgeted, irritated at the intentional delay.

"This wouldn't have to do with Dr. Young, would it? I'm not stupid, Greg. I didn't get here by being unobservant." He folded his hands over his stomach.

Shaw sunk into the worn chairs in front of Mancini's desk. "That obvious, Tom?"

"As a kick in the teeth. How's Carol and the kids?" He reached into his desk drawer, removing two crystal tumblers and a bottle of Scotch. "Off the clock now." Pouring a few fingers into each, he handed one across to Shaw.

"Gone. Left me, took the kids. Don't have the will to fight her on it as the divorce is gonna be pretty straight forward. Can't say I didn't see it coming. There's been nothing between me and her for a long time." He swirled the liquid in the glass before taking a sip.

Mancini studied him. "And Dr. Young?"

Shaw felt the warmth in his neck. "Uh…I know her from the ICU at Lakeland. We met about four years ago when there was a troublesome patient on the ward. We talk now and again, but…yeah. You know, Tom, I may be too close to this one, stepping out of bounds."

"An apt observation. However, I can see you being protective of her. I trust you have a good reason for wanting to be on the detail?"

"She's attending as Edward Haversham's date."

Mancini frowned, the lines around his eyes deepening. "You think she may gain unintentional insight to our investigation. Does she know…? Never mind. I imagine she does. Right, here's what I'm gonna do, Greg. I'll grant your request, but don't do anything stupid. This is more than your ass on the line here."

Shaw downed the rest of the drink. "Thanks, Tom. You won't regret this."

"Where've I heard that bullshit line before?"

18

The glitz of the lavishly, yet tastefully decorated residence of the mayor had Lindsay's breath catching in her throat. She felt very much the proverbial princess, swept up by her Prince Charming in a carriage pulled by gleaming white horses. She wasn't entirely sure, though, if Edward qualified as a charming prince. However, her senses were not dulled enough to prevent her from having her eyes open, and mind alert, to everything occurring.

She had almost drawn the line at Edward coming in to meet her mother and son. Something in the back of her head still urged caution. Maybe it was on account of Taylor's father. However, at his gentle urging, she relented. Taylor had stood, wide-eyed, while her mother had fawned and fluttered her hands. The entire scene had almost made her laugh and cry concurrently. Luckily, Edward didn't stay long, and soon they were off, leaving her mother and son waving from the doorway.

Taylor's father had been a wild fling while she was in medical school. The stress of examinations, dissections, and competing with classmates had led to the impulsive encounter in a janitor's closet outside one of the dissection suites. It wasn't romantic or planned—merely a way to blow off some steam. Who would have thought she'd be in that tiny percentile where the birth control pill failed?

Her plans at revealing the situation had been stalled when she saw him outside his apartment with a woman, the street lights glinting off a garish engagement ring on her left hand. Wisely choosing to remain silent, as opposed to being labeled 'that woman,' she confided in her mother, who was delighted, concerned, and supportive. Nine months later, she took a semester off, and had Taylor.

At a low point, Lindsay had eventually sent an email to his father, confessing all. The response shattered all her expectations of men. He'd told her she was a whore and a slut. And she shouldn't have opened her legs. And he wanted a DNA test. Face red and smarting, she had quietly deleted the email, vowing that Taylor only needed her and her mother to be raised properly. She had hoped at the time her decision had been the right one. The man would only resent the reminder of his infidelity and Taylor did not deserve that stigma.

As they rode in the limo to the event, Lindsay had found herself drowning out the dull drone of conversation. Edward's partner from the firm had accompanied them, along with the exotic woman from their office. She found the pairing perplexing, but it wasn't her place to question Mr. Wilks' choice of companions.

"Lindsay?" Edward's hand fell over hers, drawing her attention back to the interior of the limo. "Would you like some champagne?"

She nodded mutely.

"You're a million miles away. Don't be nervous. I wouldn't have asked you if I didn't think you'd impress." His breath was warm against her neck as he leaned in and whispered.

She accepted the glass of champagne, and relaxed back into the butter-soft leather seat. "I'm sorry, I'm usually more composed."

His fingers curled around hers. "You are, my dear." He lifted her hand, and kissed it. "We're almost there anyway."

Swallowing a liberal amount of the expensive champagne, the bubbles tickled the back of her nose and throat. She hadn't dated anyone since the catastrophe with Taylor's father. Is that why she was acting like a mindless drone? Reminding herself that this was an opportunity for networking, Lindsay calmed her nerves as they arrived, the limo pulling into line seamlessly behind many others.

***

Digging a finger under the collar of his dress shirt, Shaw swallowed hard, scowling at the scratchy, starched material. They were experiencing an unseasonably warm spell of weather, and while that might have boded well for the trick-or-treaters in a few nights, it was hell on Shaw, pools of sweat settling at the base of his spine, and dampening the fabric.

His earpiece buzzed to life. "Itchy as hell, isn't it, sir?"

How Reynolds had managed to get onto the security detail as well baffled Shaw, but he had an inkling it had something to do with keeping tabs on him. He should have been resentful, but instead, he was grateful. Reynolds held him in check, making sure he didn't let things grow too personal.

Speaking into the mic embedded in the cufflink of the shirt, Shaw felt much like 007. "Yeah, it's shit."

"Suits you, sir, if you don't mind me saying."

"Trying to shove me off to the Feds and steal my job, rookie?"

The momentary lapse of dead air had Shaw chuckling.
"No! I only meant…"

"Chill, Reynolds. Let's clear the airway."

Shaw managed to get a position patrolling the perimeter, while Reynolds was up by the front door, next to the valet. Limos and town cars had already started pulling up at the palatial residence of Mayor Bridges. Helping the foster children of the city was sure to attract all sorts of big-wigs, looking to attach their names and faces to such a noble cause, most likely to draw attention away from some of their underhanded dealings with the criminal underground. Shaw was under no delusions about the workings of politics in their city, let alone the country. However, he wasn't there to think about that, but to potentially trap a killer.

From his vantage point, he could make out the arrival of Haversham and Wilks, with their respective dates, exiting their limo. He had to blink to clear his vision as he focused on Lindsay, her hair cascading in soft curls down her back, jewelry sparkling as it caught the light from the iron lanterns hanging from the roof. He'd bet his retirement fund they were real diamonds, no doubt supplied by Haversham. He watched as they added the requisite masks required for the theme of the ball.

"Reynolds, did you run a background on this shitbag Haversham?" Shaw watched as the couple entered the mansion.

"Uh, yeah, a brief one."

"Remind me of the particulars."

There was a small pause before Reynolds spoke again, "Born and raised in Oakland, he did exceptionally well in school. No record. Accepted to Harvard with all the honors and scholarships. Came back to California to sit the bar exam, passed on the first try, no mean feat. Hired almost immediately with Wilks and Baxter, as it was known back then. Interesting working-class background, sir. His parents died in a car accident, and he was brought up by his widowed grandmother, who passed away about five years ago. Does the occasional pro-bono work, as required by his firm. That's about it. He's squeaky clean, sir."

"Squeaky clean," Shaw muttered to himself. "Thanks,

Reynolds. Keep your eyes peeled." When he looked back to where Haversham and Lindsay had been, they were gone, and a new limo had pulled up in place of theirs. "Fuck."

***

Edward took immense delight in circling the room with Lindsay on his arm. The elite were there that evening, allowing plenty of opportunities to cement his place in this upper level of society. Lindsay was sublime, captivating everyone she met. Her beauty and grace were only emphasized by her intelligence, and Edward smugly watched expressions of shock, then joy as they realized she wasn't a stereotypical airhead blonde, and perfectly capable of discussing the most complex of issues.

During a temporary lull in the conversation and introductions, Edward leaned in, inhaling her lovely fragrance, and murmuring, "You are simply magnificent, my dear."

She blushed and smiled at him. "You're flattering me, Edward."

"I never flatter." He rested a hand over hers, which was curved over the crook of his arm.

Of course, that was a blatant lie. Edward routinely used flattery to win over clients and charm investors. However, in this particular case, he spoke nothing but the truth. In the moments he picked up snippets of her chatting to the crème de la crème, he recognized a distinct passion for helping to better the community at large. Wilks had mentioned to Edward on more than one occasion in their long friendship that he would excel in politics, perhaps would even ascend to one of the Houses of government, if he were so inclined, but Edward had always brushed this off. He was satisfied with his vocation. However, hearing Lindsay speak and charm—almost as well as he did—made him reconsider this career path, and her position at his side as more than a passing fancy.

His attraction to her was never in question. After all, most are drawn to another out of lust, rather than love. She had a complicated past, it seemed, but he would find out about that before any big decisions were made. A prenuptial agreement would definitely be a requirement, as he could not be certain she might change her mind, and strip him bare of all his assets. Lindsay didn't seem like the type to be so callous, but he had been fooled before. Yes, it was time to lay his cards on the table for her and see what she had to say.

Snagging two glasses of champagne from a polished silver tray, Edward briefly made eye contact with the chief of police, Harrison Brady, identifiable from his dress uniform. His stomach did a flip at the cold expression from behind the no-doubt reluctantly donned mask. Surely the man did not still hold a grudge against his firm for their representation of Freddy Jones? They had performed their service, and had been paid well for it. After all, everyone was innocent until proven guilty. He broke the deadlocked stare, determined not to let the man put a damper on his evening.

Passing the glass to Lindsay, he guided her away from the group of people she had been conversing with, much to their chagrin. "Shall we indulge in the buffet, my dear?"

She leaned up, brushing her lips over his cheek. "I'm having a great time, Edward. I'm glad you convinced me to come."

His stomach somersaulted again, but this time, it was from complete happiness. His mind drifted as they laid their canapés on china plates and retired to a small table. Immediately, Lindsay's attention was drawn by another of the donors to the cause, discussing the medical needs of children in foster care, but he didn't mind.

There had been a time when such fine food was out of reach for him. Growing up had been a struggle, no doubt there, but his grandmother had been a good woman. She had always had money for him to participate in clubs and activities to expand on and strengthen his abilities. He had never questioned it, preferring to focus on his education. Edward knew people thought of him as an egotistical, spoiled man, but that was far from the truth, really. He'd made sure his grandmother had had the best of care later in life. Still, even going through her financial records upon her death, he had been unable to find any way to trace the large sums of money which had gone into her bank account every month. It was something which still niggled at him, usually late at night when he was in bed, trying to sleep.

"Edward?"

Blinking a few times, he plastered on his trademark dazzling smile. "Yes, my dear?"

"I was just asking if you wanted to maybe dance?"

"My darling, it would be my utmost pleasure." Rising and extending his hand, he guided her to the floor to join the whirling couples.

***

The musical selection was sublime, he thought to himself as he circled the room, the narrow flute full of champagne between his slender fingers. How lovely to see his city's finest showing up for such a worthy cause. After all, it was their duty to look after the unfortunate souls of the city.

A vision in midnight blue crossed his path, her blonde hair appearing as soft as the finest silk. He made a mental note to engage in conversation with her, perhaps later in the evening over a waltz.

19

Lindsay recognized the musical composition played by the small orchestra positioned above the polished dance floor. She thought it odd they would choose a piece from the Nutcracker at a Halloween-style function. However, the simple tune reminded her of the times she had gone to see the ballet with her mother, back when she thought the only thing worth doing in life was being a prima ballerina with the San Francisco Ballet Company.

"Pardon me. Would you care to dance?"

Lindsay lifted her head. Edward had gone to speak to a few clients, but she almost expected it would be him requesting her hand for a second time. "Why I…" She focused on the simple black mask, leaving only the man's eyes boring into her. "I'm sorry, have we met?"

"No, *ma chérie*, but you are quite the vision."

Before she could object, his hand had encircled hers and she was being led out onto the dance floor, amidst a few other couples. The mysterious man's hand encircled her waist, and he fell into the smooth steps of the dance.

"An…interesting choice of song, don't you think?" Lindsay murmured, for lack of a better conversation topic.

"Ah, yes, Tchaikovsky's *Valzer dei Fiori*, one of my favorites. Do you like it?"

"I'm sorry?" Lindsay's brow furrowed in confusion.

"The *Waltz of the Flowers*, chérie."

"Oh, yes, it's lovely."

"It's a wonderful thing, the mayor is doing, do you not agree?" His voice was muffled by the mask.

Lindsay nodded. "Yes, I find helping the less fortunate to be quite a noble endeavor."

"And if they don't deserve that help?"

She was taken aback by the rather harsh conjecture. "I believe everyone has some redeeming qualities."

"Even killers and rapists?"

She would have pulled away, but his grip tightened ever so subtly, sending her heart rate rising rapidly. "Yes…they might have had a misguided childhood, or something impacting them to make them believe there was no other path afforded to them, except crime."

Silence lapsed over them, but Lindsay's awareness heightened at each gentle application of pressure by her partner's guiding hand.

"I'm sorry, but who…" Her question was interrupted by the screams of a woman echoing in the ballroom. The orchestra came to an abrupt stop, and Lindsay stepped away from her partner to see what the commotion was about.

"I wonder…" She turned back to find her partner had vanished into the crowd of masked faces.

"Is there a doctor here?" A man had taken charge of the situation. "Please?"

Lindsay stepped forward, removing her mask. "I'm a doctor." She looked again for her dancing companion, but he was well and truly gone.

"Come this way, please." His hand encircled her elbow, tugging her past the blank faces. A few had taken off their masks, faces a mix of shock and curiosity, wondering what had happened.

Security staff parted, allowing them past, but barring the rest of the guests from leaving the ballroom. Lindsay was taken up a flight of stairs to a large mahogany door.

"Doctor, please prepare yourself." The man pushed it open.

Inside the room stood a middle-aged woman in white, her hands trembling uncontrollably. "I only came to get him for the speeches...please...what's wrong with him?"

A man Lindsay recognized as the mayor lay slumped over on his desk, eyes wide, breathing shallow. Her professional demeanor took over. "Has someone called 911?"

"No," the man answered. "The press..."

"Fu...Damn the press." Lindsay moved swiftly to the mayor, pressing her fingers to his neck. "Pulse is weak. He needs a hospital."

"But it's an election year..."

"Look, do you care that much about an election that you're willing to let him die?" Lindsay focused her attention back on her patient. "Sir...sir, can you hear me?" She yelped as her finger came into contact with a liquid on the man's neck. It burned her skin. "Get an ambulance, now!"

"Yes, fine." The man left the room.

Lindsay focused on the woman. "I need a sink." She motioned to the mini-bar in the office and Lindsay hurried over, washing her skin. She felt a soapy residue, and kept washing until it vanished. She'd taken enough labs to know what to do to neutralize something on her skin.

"Linds?"

She turned to see Shaw standing in the doorway. "What are you doing here?"

"Security detail. I was by the front door when this guy came out requesting a secret ambulance. What's going on?" He surveyed the room, seeing the mayor. "Shit!"

"Shit is right. He's got something on his neck. I didn't inspect it closely, but it burns to the touch." She extended her finger for his inspection, the skin red from the substance and cleaning.

His eyebrows furrowed, obviously drawing conclusions in his head. "I think I know what's happened."

Mrs. Bridges, who had been paralyzed up until that moment, finally spoke up. "What happened? Please."

Shaw turned. "Did you see anyone in the room when you found your husband, Mrs. Bridges?"

It made sense he would know the wife of the mayor on sight, Lindsay surmised.

"No, I came in, and he was slumped down. I may have called out as I came down the hallway."

The questioning was interrupted by the entrance of two paramedics. They hurried over to Mayor Bridges, starting to take vitals. Lindsay stood back and watched, after having given relevant information to the paramedics, her curiosity battering against the inside of her skull. What the hell was going on?

The paramedics attempted to place him onto the gurney, and a blare of alarms sounded. They pulled out the portable AED and attached it. Mrs. Bridges began to scream again, and Lindsay went to her side, holding onto the distraught woman. The solid toned beep indicated their worst fear. The mayor was dead.

20

Edward swept his gaze over the ballroom, looking for Lindsay. Amidst the budding panic about the screams, she had disappeared. He located Wilks and Zahra by the refreshment table, masks dangling from their fingertips.

"Have you seen Lindsay?"

Zahra gave him a non-committal shrug, her eyes unconcerned with the location of his date.

"Sorry, my boy, I haven't. Do you know what's going on?" Wilks peered around, giving his Phantom of the Opera style mask a twirl on his finger.

"No, but I'm going to find out." Edward crossed the floor to the doorway where two security staff stood. He made to push past them.

"Sorry, sir. We've been asked to keep everyone confined to the ballroom."

"This is an outrage! I…" Over the broad shoulder of the guard, he made out Lindsay, and she wasn't alone. He recognized the detective who had interrogated him at his office about Holzer and Jones. He touched Lindsay on the shoulder, and looked at her finger before ushering her out of the house.

Edward wanted to call out, but chose to step back, doing his best to ignore the budding irritation in his chest. Before the chaos, he had been seeking her out to divulge his intentions, and she had left with someone else. Did he know she knew Shaw? He filtered through his memory, and couldn't remember if she had mentioned him. He returned to Wilks as another officer, Shaw's lackey, entered the ballroom.

"Ladies and gentlemen, we appreciate your patience, but we ask you please bear with us. We will need to question you all about your whereabouts in this house for the past few hours."

There was a murmur of voices drowning out the young officer, and a few more uniformed cops joined him in the ballroom.

"We'll…" He had to shout to be heard, "We'll try to have you out of here as quickly as possible."

Finding a seat in the corner of the room, Edward glowered at the scene, repeating in his mind Lindsay's departure. He hoped she would have a good explanation.

Shaw knew he probably should have left Lindsay inside the mansion to be questioned along with the other guests, but his concern for her safety overwhelmed him. If he was right, they had just encountered another victim of their serial killer. Whether the wife had interrupted him, or he had planned to have the body found was something Shaw would have to deduce later.

His truck was parked on the street, and it was a good walk down the driveway. Lindsay didn't complain, despite being in heels, however, she continually glanced over her shoulder at the reflection of the blue and red lights in the trees.

"I guess they realized there was no point in worrying about an election." Her soft, matter-of-fact voice finally permeated the silence.

"Huh?" Shaw paused, bringing her around to face him.

"That's why they didn't call an ambulance right away. Bridges' personal assistant, I assume, said the press would be bad for an election year."

Shaw filed away this crumb of information, reminding himself to question the personal assistant later, after he had taken Lindsay to safety. Removing a witness from a murder scene could have him fired, but there was something about having her remain there, with the killer potentially among the guests, that made him forgo his better judgment.

"You told me you're investigating these types of murders, right?" After a few more feet of walking, she spoke again.

"Yeah." He rubbed his forehead, then loosened the ridiculous bow tie as he walked. "I am."

"Shouldn't you be back there?"

"My partner'll handle it."

She sighed. "I really should have told Edward I was leaving…"

"No!" His outburst surprised the both of them, and Lindsay stopped walking. "No, you shouldn't tell him anything. Ever. Stay away from him entirely."

Her expression, even in the low light, mixed between defiance and submission. "Why, Greg? You told me this before, but I need a valid reason. Please."

"I can't give you one. Call it instinct, call it being protective, call it whatever the fuck you want, but there is something about that guy I can't quite place my finger on." He didn't wait for an answer, but kept walking. After a few moments, he heard Lindsay resume her pace behind him, and he was thankful she chose not to ask him anymore questions. He had to talk to Mancini and explain his actions, but getting reamed by his boss could wait.

Interesting development, he thought, as he watched Detective Shaw and Dr. Young through the large bay window at the side of the house. A pity. He had really enjoyed dancing with the woman. Too bad the untimely interruption of the discovery of the mayor's body had disturbed that. He had planned for the mayor's wife to find the body of her supposedly beloved husband. She could have joined him, true enough—for her own crimes were no less noble—however, they paled in comparison to Mayor Bridges' corrupt ways.

He watched the huddled masses, women crying for a man they thought was a pillar of the community, men red-faced and outraged at the disturbance of the evening and the law enforcement presence. Finally, he spied Edward Haversham, standing with the secretary from his law firm. It surprised him that for an intelligent man, Haversham was entirely oblivious to the obvious right before his eyes. Perhaps it was finally time to enlighten him as to his true origins, and societal elevation.

Part III:

Finale

21

For once, the ward was quiet. Lindsay performed the requisite checks on the patients, noting stats and conversing with any family visitors about treatment plans. As she exited the final patient's room, her mind drifted back to the charity masquerade at the mayor's home…well, the former mayor. The city council had elected an interim mayor in the meantime, but the circumstances of Mayor Bridges' death still rattled her. The acid burns on her fingertips were evidence of something far worse going on in the city.

She leaned against the wall at the end of the ward, staring at the sparsely populated corridor. She hated not knowing the answers to the questions swimming around in her mind. There was no doubt about it—she would need to pin Greg down, and get some answers.

"Dr. Young? We have an emergency coming in. Multiple vehicle collision." A nurse hurried down the hallway toward her, blonde hair fluttering.

Lindsay perked up. As tragic as it was, the flurry of activity would keep her mind off everything until she could speak to Greg and, as predicted, the routine movements of triage, care, and finally, settling the patients onto the ward re-centered Lindsay. By the end of her shift, she was exhausted and ready to go home to a glass of wine, her son, and some trash TV.

***

Taylor was viciously coloring at the table, using his red crayon liberally.

"Whatcha up to, sweet pea?" Lindsay sat down next to her son.

"Colorin'. There's been a horrible car crash."

A cold chill settled into Lindsay's spine, before she reminded herself that little boys often were fascinated with car crashes, having seen Taylor recreate some spectacular ones with his Matchbox cars. "Oh? Is everyone okay?"

"No, the man said there were three people hurt." He picked up his black crayon and carefully drew in three stick figures amidst the red 'blood.'

Lindsay's heart began to thud. "What…man?"

"The man at the park. He talked to me until Grandma said we had to go."

"You shouldn't talk to strangers, honey." She wrapped an arm around his shoulders, holding him tightly until he squirmed away.

"Was just a story, Mommy. He said."

Suddenly, all the questions about the mayor, as well as the other people who had died under strange circumstances came flooding back to her. "I have to make a phone call. Are you gonna be okay?"

Taylor nodded, making engine noises as he continued to add details to his picture.

Lindsay hurried to retrieve her phone from her purse. She punched in Greg's number, and he answered on the first ring.

"Linds? You okay?"

"Greg, I think we need to talk…about everything. I

know it's not policy to talk about ongoing investigations, but I think there are things I need to know, especially after this past weekend…" She sighed deeply, trailing off.

"Actually, I think you're right. You still need to be interviewed about the mayor's death, and I do owe you an explanation." He sounded resigned, as if there was no other choice in the matter. "Can you meet me in about an hour? There's a pizza place on University Avenue…Pizza My Heart."

"Yeah, I know it. I'll shower and change and see you there soon." She hung up the phone as Sandra came into the room. "I'm…"

"Going out." She smiled understandingly. "Edward?"

"No, Greg."

Sandra's brow shot up. "Oh?"

"Yes, Mom, no comments from the peanut gallery." She kissed Taylor on the head, and climbed the stairs to a chorus of her mother's laughter.

***

Shaw squirmed on the red leather booth seat. He could find himself up shit creek without a paddle once he told Lindsay everything about the cases they were investigating. She was a civilian, for fuck's sake. There was no reason he should feel obligated to answer any of her questions—but he did. He'd left Reynolds sifting through the witness statements from the events of the charity ball, informing him that he was going to get more details from the doctor who had been called in to confirm the death.

"Maybe I should come with you," Reynolds had offered, his eagerness to sink his teeth into this investigation all too evident.

Shaw had declined, saying it was better he put his skills to use organizing the timeline of events, and where all the guests had fit into them. He had made the job sound much more exciting than it really was, but, still, Reynolds had complied like an eager pup wanting to please his master.

When Lindsay finally emerged through the door, Shaw watched her eyes skim the room, almost hoping she would pass right over him and decide it wasn't worth knowing any more about his case. However, he was in no such luck. With a small smile and wave, she made her way to the booth and slid in opposite him.

They exchanged the customary greetings, starting to speak at the same time with, "How are you?" Nervous laughter followed.

"Go ahead, Greg, sorry."

"Uh, yeah, not too bad. The kids are flying out for Thanksgiving, I found out. Not sure what I'm gonna do with them for a four-day weekend, but hey, can't complain, can I?"

Lindsay shook her head. "Nope. I can't believe it's almost Thanksgiving...then it'll be Christmas..."

The banal conversation trickled out, as if each was wanting to get on with the matter at hand, but reluctant to broach the subject.

"I suppose I'll ask outright. What's going on with Edward?"

Shaw swallowed. "I could get in the shit for this...but I know you'll keep confidentiality, right?" It was almost a plea.

"Of course."

"Wilks and Haversham have been indirectly involved with several cases I've been working on. They represented Freddy Jones' father in the matter of his rehabilitation, and they were representing William Holzer, the drug dealer who wound up dead. In both these cases, the victims ended up being killed with an injection of hydrochloric acid to the neck. There is also a third case, involving Dwayne Marshall, the suspected assailant of Corrine Evans, Dwayne Marshall, although the circumstances of his death—and subsequent disposal—were different from that of Jones and Holzer…"

Shaw drew a breath, knowing he had splurted out all the information rapidly. "Should we get some drinks before I continue?" He knew his own mouth was going dry, not just from speaking, but from the nature of the discussion.

Lindsay agreed, and he went to the counter, returning with two Cokes.

"Anyway, the circumstances of the mayor's death mimic those of the other three, however, the body was dumped in a prominent place. We think we have a serial killer on our hands, but he's changed his *modus operandi*, which does often happen when the need arises. The first two bodies, Holzer and Jones, were left in the same place, while Marshall and Bridges were left where they would make the most impact. We still feel there might have been an interruption with Bridges, but we can't say for certain." Shaw took a long drink of his Coke. "Are you following me?"

Lindsay's expression remained neutral. "I think so."

"Now, in all cases, except Bridges, that we know of, the victim has had some sort of…criminal past, if you will? Marshall was a suspect in the Evans case, but we could never prove his involvement. My partner is following up on everything. The guy's crazy dedicated to the job. I hope he doesn't burn out."

Lindsay swirled her straw in her glass, watching the ice spin. "So, you think Marshall was the one who hurt that little girl?"

Shaw frowned. "I'm not entirely sure, Linds. We interviewed him in the course of the investigation, but things were so hectic… My captain is starting to wonder if we missed the obvious, because we were so focused on finding the girl alive. When we did, we didn't think to follow up, because we hoped she would be able to tell us all the missing pieces. Upon reflection, it was completely crap police work."

Lindsay reached over, touching his arm. "Don't beat yourself up, Greg. I know from experience at the hospital that when tensions get high, people forget the basic procedures. It's human nature. No one is to blame."

He placed his hand over hers. "I know, but you can't make these mistakes in this line of work. The public, and the media, crucify you for it. Damned reporters."

"Have you told the Evans' family your findings?"

Shaw sighed, withdrawing his hand. "I know we'll have to. We'll have to tell them we fucked up, but hell if I want to. The Cap will make an example."

Silence settled between them.

"So where does this all leave me?" Lindsay finally asked.

Shaw stared down into his drink, watching the carbonated bubbles pop at the surface. "That depends on how close you and Haversham are."

"I haven't really spoken to him since the masquerade ball, nor he to me. I wanted to text him to apologize for abandoning him, but I wanted to talk to you first."

"I can't say for certain he has anything to do with this, Linds." He reached across the table, touching her hand. "But I want you to protect yourself, and maybe not tie yourself down to a man who is so clearly into his work for the status it gives him."

Lindsay's eyebrows shot up. "Greg, is there something more going on here? I mean, we've known each other casually for a while, and…"

He cut her off. "I respect you greatly, and your abilities as a doctor, and…" He rubbed his hand over the back of his neck. "Okay, maybe there's some attraction there, but I was married before, and now, I don't think you'd be interested in some middle-aged detective."

Her serious expression broke. "Greg, I've always had a fondness for you too, but—like you said—you were married, and then I became involved with Edward."

Shaw's face split into a boyish grin. "Well, since the marriage thing has gone to the shitter, can I interest you in dinner and a movie?"

"Should you really be cavorting with witnesses in an open case?" she teased, her eyes brightening.

"I'll take the risk. Now, is there anything else you want to ask?"

Lindsay indicated in the negative. "Although, the big bugbear in the room is still Edward. It's been nice being spoiled by a handsome man…" She laughed as Shaw made a disgruntled face. "But I don't think he's really for me. I'll text him to meet for coffee later in the week, and break things off. No use dragging something on that isn't going to work."

Shaw felt a weight lifted off his chest for the first time since Carol had told him about leaving with the kids. There was hope for the future. "Okay, pizza. Pepperoni?"

✱✱✱

The flickering fluorescent bulbs cast an eerie pallor over the interior of the sterilized laboratory suite. A redheaded man in a white lab coat gave off the impression of a newborn colt, his knees knocking together searching for his mother for some sort of protection from the man in front of him.

"I can't do this anymore. My supervisors are going to start to notice things missing from the lab when they do their inventory," the skinny man whined, making him all the more distasteful in his eyes. How he had ever seen fit to assist this worm was beyond him.

"You knew our agreement, Mr. Bailey. I get you acquitted on those *horrible* statutory rape charges, and you're entirely in my debt. Now, I would like my supplies, please." He held out a gloved hand, growing increasingly irritated with the delays.

Reluctantly, Bailey placed the case of syringes and the vial of hydrochloric acid into his waiting hand. "And if I lose my job?"

"Well, that would be very unfortunate indeed, Mr. Bailey. Very unfortunate." He smiled. This was certainly his favorite part of these exchanges—watching his unwilling victim squirm.

"I can't help it if that happens!"

"And I can't help if evidence reaches the police of your other endeavors, Mr. Bailey." He spun on a polished heel and strode away, unable to cope with the sniveling any longer. The man was not worthy of his attention. He would have to look at other means of acquiring his supplies in the future, then he could rid himself of the troublesome Mr. Bailey.

22

Reynolds was sitting at his desktop computer when Shaw returned from his meeting with Lindsay. He whistled, uncharacteristically happy under the circumstances, but he felt he deserved it. It had been a long time since anything good had happened.

"All okay with the witness, sir?" Reynolds peeked up, his fingers stopping on the keyboard.

"Fantastic, son. What have you got?"

Just as those words were spoken, a mail room clerk dropped a manila envelope on the desk and continued on, his cart squeaking. Shaw scooped it up, flipping it over to see who had sent it. No return address, but it was c/o Detective Gregory Shaw. Shrugging, he opened it and a few photographs spilled out, along with a note:

Marshall paid off his alibi. I expected more from you, Detective.

"Holy fuck!" Shaw quickly grabbed an evidence bag and a pair of gloves from his desk drawer, and placed the paperwork inside.

Reynolds leaned over to see what the commotion was about.

"We need to get the person from the Evans case in

here, the one who alibied Marshall. Pull up the original interview. It was a woman, if I remember correctly." Of course he remembered every nuance of the case. The woman had had track marks up and down her arms, scratching like crazy, as if there were hundreds of bugs under her skin—the result of methamphetamine addiction. She'd been jittering her leg so badly, it had caused his pen to bounce like the needle on a seismograph.

"On it, sir."

Shaw gaped at the photographs showing Marshall talking to their witness, and handing over money. How the hell had someone gotten these? This was getting all too fishy for his liking. Too many coincidences, not enough reasonable explanations.

"Got it."

"Last known whereabouts?"

Reynolds' face dropped.

"What is it?"

"Dead, sir. Her body was found by a homeless guy. OD'd."

Shaw slumped into his chair. "Before you ask why we accepted the alibi of some druggie, we had security cameras to back it up. We saw her go into the hotel with Marshall. The clerk backed it up that he'd been in there all night. We had nothing to hold him on." He leaned on his elbows, hands in his hair. "I don't know why at the time, but it was combined with the search for Corrine… Fuck. Mancini's gonna have my head for breakfast."

"What's going on now? I have a dead mayor, and a string of unsolved homicides. What could you possibly do to make my day any worse?"

Shaw slowly lifted his head, looking up at his captain. "The witness who provided Marshall's alibi in the Evans case was paid off to give the statement."

Mancini's hand hit the desk hard, causing Shaw and Reynolds to jump. "Fuckin' hell! When was it given?"

"While we were still looking for Corrine."

Reynolds piped up, his voice squeaking, "Yeah, sir, the recording corroborates…"

At Mancini's glare, Reynolds shut up and averted his eyes. "The commissioner was very close with the mayor. He wants a resolution to this fast, before the press start reporting on the incompetence of our police force. Re-interview the mayor's wife. I wasn't a massive fan of Bridges, but he was a crowd pleaser. Always felt something wasn't right about him."

Shaw and Reynolds remained static.

"Now! Before I get my balls handed to me on a plate!"

Lindsay returned home to silence. Her mother and Taylor must have gone to bed. She went into the dark living room and sat on the couch, not bothering to flip on the light. What had she seen in Edward? He was flattering, yes, but she had been flattered by men before. He had also lied to her about his motives. At the time, she had been amused by his ploy, but now, with all that Greg had said, was he really that innocently charming?

Withdrawing her phone from her pocket, she stared at the screen. She knew she had to text Edward and let him go. It wasn't fair to string someone along. Granted, he had always made her feel like she was a princess—spoiled and held on a pedestal—but there was never that level of comfort she experienced with Greg. Hitting the button on the side of her phone, it sprung to life. She scrolled through the contacts and located Edward's name.

Sorry for the other night. Things got complicated quickly. Can we meet for coffee?

The response pinged back not a few moments later.

Don't apologize. When? E.H.

Lindsay gnawed on the inside of her cheek, trying to remember her schedule.

Free Friday. See you then?
Until then. E.H.

As she held the phone, she watched the screen dim, then blacken after reading the message. She recalled something Greg had mentioned, about being unable to get any information out of Haversham or Wilks regarding the coincidence of them being involved with nearly all the victims. Lindsay knew she wasn't a police officer, and getting involved could be dangerous for her...and maybe Taylor. However, if she could manage to steer the conversation in that direction, what harm could it do if Edward slipped up and said something which might be of use to Greg?

"Mommy?" Taylor stood in the archway to the living room, rubbing his eyes.

"Hey, bug, what are you doing up?"

"Nightmares."

Lindsay got up and scooped her little boy up, snuggling him close. "It's not real. Come on, I'll tuck you back into bed." As she climbed the stairs, a strange thought crossed her mind. Maybe nightmares were more real than she wanted to admit.

***

After the charity ball, he knew he needed to have a break from the adrenaline vibrating in his veins. A night at the symphony would do just that. He had a box specifically reserved for his own use. Sometimes, he was accompanied by a lovely lady, usually a paid escort, whom he would charm with the most exquisite of treats—champagne and chocolates—until she was quite pliable. He wasn't a man driven by baser instincts; he knew how to restrain himself from giving into temptation. The women, on the other hand, were gagging for it by the time the performance was over, and who was he to disappoint them? A quick fumble in the back of the limo, and they would be set out, satisfied, dreaming of something out of *Pretty Woman*. Pathetic. However, at least they were honest about their profession.

He thought of the mayor, dipping his hand in the kitty, so to speak. Weakness could not be tolerated. One must be in control at all times. Addiction was the height of imperfection, and a taint on his city…no, his world. However, he felt hypocritical. He was addicted—in a way—to killing off the undesirables, but he felt a sense of pride at his accomplishments. All other addicts only found themselves in an endless cycle of despair.

The limo pulled up outside the symphony hall and he alighted, ascending the steps to the epitome of culture, in his mind. There was a lovely harpist taking center stage that evening, something he would not have missed for anything. Playing the harp took immense talent and dexterity, a skill which was honed through years of practice, much like his own experiences. One must experience to succeed in anything.

His box was appointed with the usual accoutrements—wine and a list of the female harpist's accomplishments. He liked to know whom he was watching and his contacts provided excellent background checks.

Gentle applause broke his reverie as he gazed down at the dark-haired woman in a fine black dress which clung to her curves. She bowed her head to the audience and sat, drawing the instrument to her shoulder like one would comfort a child. Her fingers met the strings and magic emerged. The music filled the hall. He spent several moments observing the subtle changes of expression in her face, and the way her fingers strummed the instrument. He admired her ability to play without sheet music, instead letting her passion lead the way. Her cheek delicately brushed the wood, and his eyes fluttered closed. Majestic.

He felt a wave of tranquility encompass him, certain of his place in this world once again. The text messages between Edward and the good doctor—obtained through his tracked phone—troubled him mildly, but he could remedy that. He would invite Edward to dinner and show him how he could better the city, beyond simple arguments before a judge. He would show him how to atone for those men he represented, who had committed the most heinous of crimes. And Edward would thank him for the gift.

The last notes of music hung in the air before she placed her hands flat against the strings. Applause again replaced music, and he clapped louder than anyone else present.

23

The invitation to visit Wilks' private residence took Edward by surprise. He had rarely been invited to his employer's home, despite the close relationship they shared. In a way, he understood. His own home was his sanctuary, and he despised it being invaded. Dressed appropriately for dinner in a gray pinstriped Hugo Boss suit, with a starched navy-blue dress shirt and silver tie, Edward was curious to see Wilks answer the door himself. He almost expected him to have staff, judging by the size of the large, appointed home.

Wilks shook his hand warmly, guiding him in. "Welcome, my boy, welcome! Come in."

Piano music filtered through the hallway, as Wilks brought him into the dining room. Edward glanced up, a neutral expression on his face, wondering how the music could disseminate so clearly throughout the home. Wilks seemed to read his mind.

"Ah, inset speakers. I couldn't be without them. That's Beethoven's *Moonlight Sonata*. Do you like it?"

Edward nodded. "It is one of my favorites, yes. I prefer piano pieces."

Wilks clapped him on the shoulder. "Ah, you see, it's the strings for me, although I am also partial to woodwinds." He wagged a finger. "I am especially fond of the harp. I find it so fascinating to watch someone play. Have you been to the symphony lately?"

Shaking his head, Edward followed Wilks to the end of a long, dark walnut table, set for two places with pristine cloth and gleaming silver. "We must remedy that, yes, we must. Exposure to classical music helps you process thought. That's why they play Mozart to babies, or some such nonsense. Sit, sit!" He gestured to one chair.

"Do you...live alone?"

Wilks nodded. "Yes, I prefer my solitude. Most evenings, I do cook for myself."

Edward's eyebrows shot up in surprise.

"Don't be so shocked, my boy, I am quite a capable man. However, on occasions where I host guests, I prefer to hire in a cook. I do have a maid who comes once a week, but I am, on the whole, a tidy man."

As he spoke, a man emerged from the kitchen in chef whites. He presented a bottle of California Zinfandel for Wilks' approval, before pouring a small measure in each glass. Setting the bottle to the side, he dismissed himself.

"There are some times only a Californian wine will do. I feel, at the moment, the French are too settled in their ways of viticulture. Also, knowing your preference for red meat, I have chosen your favorite for tonight's dinner— filet mignon. I hope it meets with your satisfaction."

The chef returned again with two plates of grilled romaine salad, topped with a drizzle of vinaigrette dressing. Edward soon understood that the chef not only cooked, but would also be their server for the evening. It was irregular, but he supposed Wilks was paying him well for the privilege. The hearts of the romaine lettuce were seared to precision, so as not to take away from the crisp chilled interior, and the dressing provided just enough tang to make the dish perfectly balanced.

The red wine seeped into Edward's limbs, relaxing him enough to start talking about the events of the charity ball. "Did anyone speak to you?"

Wilks tapped his fork against the plate for a few seconds. "Yes, they did."

"Interesting. I wasn't interviewed."

"No, my boy, I assured them you had been in the ballroom the entire evening with the lovely Dr. Young. She certainly has provided you with worthy distraction, am I right?"

Edward nearly choked on his salad. "I find her to be wonderful company, but we have not progressed beyond that…if that's what you're saying…"

"Ah, I see." Wilks was expressing more interest than Edward thought necessary in his romantic life.

"I would like to take things further with her, and I had contemplated telling her so at the ball, but she left before I could. I'm hoping to make my wishes known when we meet later this week for coffee."

The fork hit Wilks' salad plate with a clatter. "What wishes?"

Edward's brow knitted, as he could not decipher why Wilks was behaving so strangely. "I wish to make things more serious between us. I feel she might be someone I could see myself spending the rest of my life with."

"She has a son, correct?"

Edward couldn't remember ever having mentioned this fact to Wilks, but he continued all the same. "Yes, Taylor. I met him the night of the ball. She lives with her mother. Taylor's father is no longer in the picture, and I believe him to be an intelligent boy, just like his mother…"

Wilks' often carefully weaved composure dropped abruptly. "This is unacceptable, Edward. The woman is tainted."

Not believing he had heard him correctly, Edward

fixed his eyes on his partner. "I'm sorry...tainted?"

"She has baggage, my boy. A son from a failed marriage? Absolutely out of the question."

A need rose in Edward to defend Lindsay from this onslaught of slander. "They were never married. It was a complicated situation." In truth, he didn't know if what he was saying bore fact, but he didn't think Lindsay would be so flippant in her actions.

"You deserve someone who is pristine. This city is too full of those with secrets...secrets that lay corruption at our very feet!"

Edward made a move to rise. This was so unlike Wilks. "I'm sorry, maybe I should leave."

"Sit!"

The sharp order came so suddenly, Edward felt he had no choice but to comply. Wilks must have realized his irrational manner and coughed, running a hand over his jacket.

"I apologize, Edward, but if you are to rise to the heights I know you are capable of, I must insist you consider how her background could come to harm you in the long run."

"I don't see how my relationship with Lindsay is any business of yours, but if you had observed her at all at the charity ball, you would see how poised and refined she is. Her intelligence is beyond compare, and she made everyone who spoke to her feel at ease. I don't understand your objections at all."

Wilks pushed his salad plate aside, folding his fingers, and resting his elbows on the table. "It is time I told you the truth about your childhood circumstances, Edward."

The interview room stank, but there was nothing that could be done about it. Reynolds wrinkled his nose as they escorted the former mayor's wife into its dank interior. She reacted much the same.

"Is there nowhere we could do this that's less…" She waved a hand, searching for the right word.

"Sorry, ma'am, but this is the only facility we have at the moment." Shaw trailed in after them, causing the pair to jump at his unannounced intrusion. "It's just a few questions, and we'll have you out of here in no time."

The two detectives sat opposite the woman, who was doing a fair impression of Jackie O after the death of JFK, only she didn't look as elegant in the pantsuit as she thought she did. Shaw sighed. This was the last thing he wanted to be doing—interviewing a grieving widow—but Mancini wanted all loose ends tied for the chief.

"So, Mrs. Bridges, can you tell us again what you were doing on the night of the charity ball?"

Reynolds hit the button of the recorder.

"As I said before, and repeatedly since then, I was coming to find my husband for the evening's speeches."

"And what was his state when you found him?"

She plucked a lace handkerchief from her bag and dabbed her eyes. "My Reggie was bent over his desk. That's when I knew something was wrong."

"And what happened after that?"

"I called for help."

Shaw shuffled through some paperwork, trying to look like he had something on her. "Did your husband have any enemies, Mrs. Bridges?"

She shook her head with another dramatic sniffle. "None that I know of. That wound on his neck, do you think that's what caused his death?"

Shaw glanced over at Reynolds, who shrugged. They hadn't released that detail to anyone, hoping to use it to wean out any false reports. "What wound?"

"The one the doctor was looking at."

So, she had been paying attention. "Ah, yes, well, we haven't conclusively ruled it out."

"The chief of police said there were other cases. Do you think someone targeted my husband?"

Shaw nearly snapped the pencil in half. The chief had no business talking to a witness in an ongoing case. "It's all under investigation. Why would someone target your husband?"

The box of a room descended into silence, only the gentle whir of the recorder making any noise at all.

"Mrs. Bridges? We need to know if your husband was into anything which might have made him any enemies. It will be kept in the strictest confidence, unless we need to use it as evidence in court."

The crocodile tears recommenced. "My Reggie was a good man. He cared for this city and the people in it…"

"But?"

"He had a gambling habit. A bad one. He…borrowed money from some of the foundations we run to pay off the debts. The masquerade was a way to recoup the losses."

"Did anyone else know about this?"

"No…maybe our lawyers? I don't know…I never dealt with any of that." She boo-hooed more, until Reynolds gave Shaw a pleading look, and he nodded.

"We will need to see any documents about this, Mrs. Bridges. Who represents your interests?"

"Oh, Wilks and Haversham. Mr. Wilks has always been so very attentive to our needs."

The pencil snapped.

24

Shaw stormed out of the interview room. There it was again! Wilks and Haversham. Yet, every time they went to question either, they got the brush off. There was something there, he was sure of it, but they were hiding behind client confidentiality. Or, maybe, they were hiding behind their own guilt? He sat at his desk, rocking side to side in the chair.

"Anything from the wife?" Mancini had emerged from his office shortly after Shaw had vacated the interview room.

Looking off to the side, Shaw watched Reynolds escort Mrs. Bridges to the elevator. Then, he directed his attention to Mancini. "Yeah…they were represented by Wilks and Haversham. The same firm who reported Holzer missing and worked for Freddy Jones' father."

"And the Evans case? Don Marshall or something?"

"Dwayne Marshall. We got something in the mail, as you know, but the techs weren't able to lift any prints. It was a bust. However, the manner of death ties the three together…as does the mayor."

"Shit, so you're saying our serial got into the mayor's

house the night of this party and killed him? How the fuck does that happen?"

Shaw felt the sarcastic response forming before he could stop it. "Cause we knew exactly who he was, and didn't think to stop him."

"This is no time for levity, Shaw! My ass, your ass, his ass..." He pointed to Reynolds as he came back. "...will all be fucked if we don't get this solved. Go back to square one. I don't want another body on my hands!" Mancini's office door slamming rattled the office.

"Your boss seems...angry."

Shaw spun in the chair, only just catching Reynolds' slack-mouthed stare. "Linds, uh, what are you doing here?"

"The guys at reception said to just come up when I said I was here to see you. Is there somewhere we can talk?"

"Yeah, yeah, uh, let's get a cup of coffee."

Together, they walked to the small staff room. Lindsay sat, while Shaw distributed coffee in two clean, but stained, mugs. "What's up?"

"I've been thinking about what you said..." she lowered her voice.

Shaw nodded quickly, glancing at the door. "Yeah?"

"What if I can help? I'm closer to Edward than you or your department are likely to get, and I..."

"Nope, out of the question, Linds. I'm not gonna put you in harm's way to satisfy a case. It would be completely unethical." He reached over and took her hand. "Besides, I care about you too much to do anything that stupid."

"Even if it would help reveal a potential connection to the murders?"

Shaw shook his head. "Nope, no deal. I appreciate the offer, but I'd like you to break up with him." He looked down at the steaming cup. "I...I'm sorry. I don't want to tell you what to do, but I hope you understand, now that I've told you what's up."

Lindsay smiled, squeezing his hand. "I understand,

Greg. Anyway, he's too high maintenance for me. Imagine having to be that social all the time! I wonder if he'd even appreciate a night on the couch with a bad movie."

Shaw laughed, feeling his heart lighten. "Yeah, probably not."

Taking a sip of the coffee, she made a face. "This tastes like sludge."

"Yeah, now you know how we feel." He stood up. "I'll…text you later to talk about that dinner and a movie thing?"

She smiled, patting him on the arm. "You do that." She walked out through the squad room, and left.

"Who was that, sir?" Reynolds was right there to meet Shaw when he came out after her.

"Dr. Lindsay Young."

"The one from the crime scene?"

"Yeah, she works at Lakeland Hospital. We know each other in passing." Shaw grumbled something about nosy kids and went back to his desk.

Reynolds tripped after him. "Soooo, you ask her out?"

"What business is it of yours, *junior*?" He slammed emphasis on the last word, trying to get him to back off.

"Just askin', sir. She seems nice and all, and with your wife now out of the picture…"

"Too far, Reynolds, too far." Still, Shaw chuckled to himself. He was happy, happier than he'd been in a long time with Carol. Maybe this was just what he needed to take his mind off the case. Then, his expression darkened. Nothing would ease his mind until he knew Lindsay was as far away from Haversham as she could get. He understood her motivation in asking him if she could help, but there was no way the department would allow it. They'd have to go through by-the-book means of gathering evidence, if they were to nail this bastard.

"Do you ever feel like maybe this guy is doing our work for us? Like, I mean, he's taking out bad guys. The world's probably a better place for them being gone." Reynolds shrugged, diverting the topic of conversation to a more philosophical one.

"I see what you're saying. There's times I'd like to shoot first, and ask questions later. I think that's human nature to want to see the bad guy punished. However, that's why we have to rely on the system, even if it's corrupt as fuck sometimes."

"I think more than one officer on the department was happy to see Freddy Jones dead," Reynolds whispered loudly, as if half the room didn't share the popular opinion.

"Jones was dirt, that's true. Doesn't mean he deserved to be killed with an injection of acid to the neck. With time, no doubt, he'd have been picked up on something. I'm under no illusions that Daddy paying for high-priced rehab would have changed shit." Shaw clicked into his email. "I wonder how fast we could get Bridges' financials, including those from any foundations they ran."

"The foundation accounts should be public record, on account of them being non-profits and all."

Shaw was moderately impressed. "Good work. I'd forgotten about that. See if you can get a copy. As for the Bridges' financial records, I think we'll need to talk to the DA. Say it'd be relevant to our case if we could trace it all back…maybe find connections to the killer? I think we can say this killer knew all the victims."

"I'd bet my money on that Haversham guy. He's worked for Wilks for a while, and he had contact with all the victims."

"True, but he seems like he'd rather keep his own skin than get it shuttled off to prison for murder."

Reynolds leaned back into his chair. "Ya think that maybe this guy thinks he's above us? Like he's smarter?"

"No shit, Sherlock. Got any other bright ideas?" Shaw smirked, and double-clicked on an email, reading about some police fund for fallen officers.

"Well…we find the connection between Marshall and the law firm. Find out if they ever represented him, or if he made any calls to lawyers when we held him in custody, regarding the Evans girl."

Shaw nodded slowly, tapping his fingers on the desk. "Never assume, but while we're on the subject, what if the killer is either Wilks or Haversham, and whichever one of them is doing the dirty work is using this pro bono defense lawyer bullshit to pick out victims?"

"So, you're saying we have to wait until the next body turns up?"

Shaw sighed, and glanced at Mancini's office door. "The Cap won't like it, but yeah, I think we will."

25

Hand frozen, fork hovering above his filet mignon, Edward struggled to absorb what Wilks had just told him. He set the utensil down. "So, you knew my parents."

"Yes, Edward, I did."

"And the car accident was no accident?"

Wilks kept a placid smile on his sharp features. "Yes."

"How did you…"

"Ah, that's the beauty of it. I maintained connections, at the time, with a rather unscrupulous young officer at the station. He would pass on my business card to anyone who might be in desperate need of representation. Only the most unsavory of crimes would do. I paid the officer enough to keep his mouth shut. Then, as my reputation grew, I found I didn't need referrals. People would come to me." Wilks appeared immensely pleased with himself.

Edward's heart rate increased. "And my father…"

"Was undeserving of the title. His crimes were numerous. Of course, your mother was an unfortunate casualty of the entire affair. Still, it made sense to mold you while you were still vulnerable. I guided you, maneuvered you in the right direction, to the right schools. I even indulged your rebellious period when you wanted to be an artist. Do you remember?"

Edward remembered. He had arranged an exhibition after a teacher told him he had real talent. After no one showed up, not even his own grandmother, he gave up the dream and returned to his studies.

"It's easy to do things when one has connections, Edward. You see, it is our duty to set an example to the greater world. If people are unwilling to follow that example, we must remove them from society."

Even Edward, despite his enjoyment of the finer things, and his dislike of unintelligent people, did not believe the best way to shape the world was to remove the people deemed to be less than acceptable to society.

"I know what you are thinking. It is a great deal to take in. Perhaps I could show you?" Wilks rose, beckoning Edward to follow him into his study.

The décor exuded wealth and power and, for a moment, Edward forgot the content of their conversation, and admired it openly. The desk was polished to a sheen, and the bookcase behind it was lined with pristine conditions of novels and legal texts.

"Beautiful, is it not? I find it allows me to concentrate better when I know the things around me are of the utmost quality." He slid *Les Misérables* from its position in the bookcase, and typed in a code on a hidden keypad. The bookcase mechanism whirred and it moved, revealing a long passageway. "Come with me." Wilks did not hesitate; he shifted into the cool corridor, expecting Edward to trail obediently.

As they walked down the sloping floor, Edward thought he could hear banging. His throat tightened as he began to understand what was about to happen. He stopped, holding out his hands. "No, Bernard, no…"

Wilks turned, smiling demonically. "But, yes, Edward. This is what you were trained for. You will take over my position and continue on as I retire. Trust me, I am doing this all for your benefit. We can look over the paperwork when we finish here." He continued on, the banging growing louder.

Edward willed his feet to move, more for self-preservation than anything. When he listened past the banging, he swore he could hear Vivaldi's *Four Seasons* concerto, the movement for *Spring*. The lively tune did not seem at all appropriate for the circumstances.

"After one of my most recent experiences, I decided installing speakers down here would make the mission a much more pleasant one, don't you agree?"

Unable to come up with any sort of response, Edward watched as Wilks used a fingerprint and retinal scanner to open another steel door. Drawing in a steadying breath, he stepped forward, taking in his surroundings. Bound to a bolted-down chair in the center of the room was a man, blindfolded and gagged. The banging must have come from him hitting his feet on the floor, however, until they entered the room, there had been no noise heard in the rest of the house.

"Soundproofing is essential to this work. Sometimes, depending on the situation, I leave them here for days before I complete my work." He handed Edward a paper suit, similar to those worn by forensic investigators. "We don't want to leave any traces on the body, do we?"

The muffled screams of the man echoed off the walls. Although his other senses were impaired, his hearing was quite intact.

"Oh, and if, perhaps, you are considering going all white knight, Edward, my boy, please bear in mind all that I have over you. Besides, who would believe you?" He primed a hypodermic syringe with liquid from a vial. "Now, shall we begin?"

Bile rose rapidly in Edward's throat. He had spent nearly two hours watching Wilks torture, and then finally put out of his misery, the man tied to the chair. When finally released from the room, with as much dignity as he could manage, Edward had asked for directions to the bathroom. Vivaldi would forever haunt his nightmares. He barely made it to the toilet in time as he voided his stomach of the extravagant meal.

Splashing cold water on his face, he struggled to remember what Wilks had said during the course of the macabre performance. The man before them had been a child abuser. Wilks did not go into the grim details of the man's crimes, but it seemed he had a penchant for small girls. While in the course of the torture, Wilks iterated very clearly his opinions on men who hurt children. The garbled screams, and the smell of burnt flesh had Edward gagging again.

Wilks was expecting him to carry on this sick act after he retired to live out his days at his vacation home. Edward was horrified. All these doors covertly opened by Wilks throughout his entire life were meant to lead to this very moment? Edward shook his head vehemently. There was no feasible way he could do any of that. Sure, he enjoyed his power and position, but to actively seek out criminals, and torture them to death? He scooped up some water, rinsing his mouth. Wilks was insane.

A knock sounded at the door. "Edward? Are you well?"

"I...can't do this, Bernard. It's insanity."

Silence loomed before Wilks spoke again. "I had worried you might say that. However, you must remember what I have over you. I did not want to do this. I had hoped you would come willingly to my side of things. But if you don't, I will see you convicted of all these cleansings I have done."

Edward's ghostly white face stared back at him from

the mirror. Wilks would blackmail him. No, surely the police would see what this was? Then, he recalled all the visits from the detectives, the unintended meetings at the hospital where Lindsay worked… Wilks could do it. That was a certainty.

"I need time to consider everything."

"Take as much time as you need, my boy. I know what your answer will be." Wilks must have left the door because all he could here was humming.

Vivaldi.

***

Wilks was immensely pleased with the outcome of his small reality check, as the youth of today called it. He had hoped Edward would have been less of a coward when it had come to his proposal, but he supposed that might have been his own fault. He had, after all, coddled the young man throughout his life. Now, he had to consider where he would dispose of his latest victim. It would be unwise to do so in one of the same locations. He smiled to himself, realizing he was about to pull off his greatest body dump to date.

There was still the matter of Dr. Lindsay Young. At first glance, he could ignore her past. Society had come a long way since the days of his parents, yet, something niggled at him. Dr. Young would be intrusive. She would figure out what Edward was doing, following in his footsteps. This would be entirely unacceptable.

Returning to the dining room, Wilks caught sight of a screen illuminating from under the table. He picked up Edward's cell phone curiously. Perhaps if he removed Dr. Young from the picture for Edward, he would understand. Yes, this was the way to go.

Opening up the text messages, he tapped out a simple one to the good doctor.

Plans changed, meet me at the office on Wednesday. E.H.

26

Spending the day with Greg had been a much-needed break from the chaos which seemed to be swirling around them. Lindsay had always enjoyed his company, but to interact with him on a much more casual level was something she found to be an even greater pleasure. He even insisted on taking Taylor along to the movie, picking a kid friendly one, even if watching Trolls dance wasn't his thing, he made the effort.

After dropping Taylor off, a half-filled bucket of popcorn in his hand and chocolate smeared on his face, he treated Lindsay to another movie and dinner, a proper date. Left at the front door with a kiss on the cheek, she knew she had made the right decision by telling Edward things were over between the pair of them—well, she would be. The peculiar text asking to meet him at his office had her raising an eyebrow, but she went with it.

Sandra was waiting up for Lindsay when she returned. "So, how was it?"

"Really great, Mom. I know Greg is still going through some stuff with his ex-wife, but he was genuinely kind today. And he treated Taylor with respect."

Passing over a glass of red wine, her mother smiled. "And your Mr. Haversham?"

Lindsay made a face, unintentionally. "He's a good man, but I think he needs someone who is willing to dedicate herself to him fully. It was nice to be spoiled, but I love my job, and Taylor is my priority. I don't know how he would fit into the greater ambitions Edward seems to have."

"When will you tell Edward?"

"In a few days. He asked me to meet him at his office on Wednesday. I shouldn't be long."

Sandra nodded, sipping the rich wine. "Excellent. I think Detective Shaw is a better match anyway. He has sense, and is very down to earth. That's the type of man I would hope you'd choose…I mean, if you had to choose. Cause you don't. You can always stay here with me."

"Oh, Mom, I'm not planning on going anywhere any time soon." She reached out, and hugged her mother tightly.

Sandra ran a hand over her daughter's blonde hair. "I hope so, sweetheart." Drawing back to arm's length, she smiled warmly. "Now, shall we catch up on some trash TV before your detective has you out every night he can?"

✶✶✶

Sleep eluded Edward. He kept flashing back to the night with Wilks to the point he phoned in sick for the following week. He would just have to text Lindsay and reschedule their talk. Cursing as he scrounged through his briefcase and his apartment, he realized that he must have left his phone at the office. Lying back on the couch, he rubbed his hand over the days' old stubble. Never before would he have let himself be so unkempt.

Wilks had brought to light memories of things Edward had hoped to forget, especially surrounding his parents. His father had always treated him with kindness, offering a piece of candy behind his mother's back before dinner. His mother smelled like citrus—a smell he found so appealing, especially in Lindsay—and fresh baked bread. He couldn't remember his parents ever having done him any disservice, or doing anything which would be constituted as illegal. Why would Wilks have seen fit to target them? How did he even find out about his parents?

Edward remembered his grandmother coming to him, after his parents had never arrived to pick him up from school. He had waited in the office, sitting on the hard, wooden bench opposite the secretary, kicking his heels against the base until she shushed him. After a few unanswered calls, she had approached the principal, a balding man with kind eyes, who searched out emergency contacts. As it happened, the police had just called his grandmother, once they had identified the possible passengers of the mangled Buick through DMV records.

She had knelt before him, blue eyes swimming with tears, gently informing him that his parents were never coming home. He remembered feeling numb, like when he'd been hit in the gut playing football on the playground. The tears had come later, in great, gulping sobs, as she had rocked him, the scent of gardenia flooding his nostrils from her perfume.

Edward sat upright on the couch, gasping for breath like he did all those years ago. Maybe that detective would be willing to help him. Maybe they could protect him…if he went to them first. However, he had to get his phone back. It held all his contacts, even those he did not want to speak to. The detective's number was stored, in case he came calling again regarding those dead clients, and Edward didn't want to answer.

Vivaldi entered his mind, and he pounded his forehead with the flat of his hand. He felt like he was going insane. He thought of all the opportunities Wilks had afforded him—the schools, the financial backing, hell, even the job.

All of it seemed to come at a higher cost than just charity. He wished his grandmother was still alive to maybe shed some light on this unlikely sponsorship, or maybe, he would just have to ask Wilks for more detail. That would be conditional on his…acceptance of Wilks' deplorable offer. Or maybe, he could accept and then take out the man responsible? Would that make him just as bad?

Going to his liquor cabinet, Edward withdrew a bottle of whisky, pouring himself a small tumbler. It wasn't often he got drunk, but he figured tonight would make a good exception.

27

As the phone blared to life on Shaw's desk, around midnight, he knew this was it. The moment they had been dreading had come. He had spent a wonderful day with Lindsay and her son, and now, the reality of the universe as he knew it was about to come crashing down. Even before the officer spoke the words, Shaw had them imprinted on his brain.

"Detective, we found another body."

Shaw let out a prolonged sigh. "Where?"

"Sir, uh, you're not gonna like this."

"Spit it out, man."

"On the chief's front lawn."

The phone dropped from Shaw's hand, and he gaped at Mancini's office door. His captain stood in the open portal, his face the color of tomato ketchup.

"Thanks." Shaw hung up the phone and stood. Reynolds scrambled to his feet next to him.

Mancini strode over to them, his neck fit to burst from his collared shirt. "What the hell is going on with this department? Never, in all my years as Captain, have I had this level of incompetence. Go see what the hell we're dealing with and then, Shaw, you're on administrative leave, by order of the chief." He returned to his office, the slamming door causing the entire squad room to jump.

"Shit, sorry, sir," Reynolds spoke after a few moments.

Shaw sat heavily in his chair. "We both know Wilks and Haversham are tied to this shit somehow. I just wish I could prove it! They're untouchable, it seems." His shoulders slumped forward. Shaw was dejected. In all his career in law enforcement, he had an unblemished record. Now, in the span of four months, his existence had started to come down around his ears.

Reynolds' hand landed lightly on his shoulder. "I'll…do my best, sir, to discover what's going on. I don't plan to let this rest…even if you aren't here to guide me."

"When are your exams, Reynolds?"

"Just before Christmas, sir."

"You'll ace 'em. Now, let's get over to the chief's house before he decides to place me on permanent leave."

The drive to the chief's residence took place in silence. Shaw appreciated Reynolds' ability to know when to speak, and when to shut up. This was a shut-up moment. All Shaw wanted to do was leave Reynolds to handle it all, and shoot off to Lindsay's house. He needed to hear her say it was okay, that he was only doing his job. For some reason, her opinion meant more to him than anyone else's right now.

Lights flashed in the distance as they turned onto the chief's street. The black coroner's van was already there. Reynolds, who had decided it best he drive, parked behind it. Both detectives got out and crossed to the yellow tape, strung from two trees at the corners of the chief's property. Standing on the porch, illuminated by pulsating red and blue lights, stood the chief, his expression somewhere between pissed off and *really* pissed off. His dark eyes reflected the scene, arms crossed firmly over his chest.

Reynolds hesitated, stopping cold in his tracks.

Placing a hand on the rookie detective's shoulder, Shaw

gave him a reassuring smile. "It's my ass they want, son. You go talk to the coroner." He lightly propelled him in the direction of Espinoza, who was bent over the corpse on the immaculately trimmed green lawn.

Inhaling, he continued his death march to the porch, wondering why Mancini was throwing them under the bus like this. Shaw knew Mancini and the chief were tight, and he also knew the death of the mayor had put everyone on a knife's edge. Still, they could only work within their means. Murder investigations, especially those concerning serials, weren't resolved overnight.

"Sir."

As Shaw stepped up the porch steps, he observed several veins threatening to burst through Chief Brady's neck. The man was struggling to maintain control.

"Shaw, do you know what it's like to be awoken to your teenage daughter coming into the house screaming her head off?"

"No, sir."

"Takes years off your life. Now, I want to know what half-assed police work is going on in my city. This will be the fourth victim, yes?"

"Fifth…sir." Shaw swallowed over the building lump in his throat, his face burning from the chief's close scrutiny.

Brady nodded stiffly, his hands clenching and unclenching at his sides. "And you've managed to keep most of it out of the press, I take it?"

"Yes, sir, we didn't want to create a city-wide panic."

"I see. So, what is your progress?"

Rubbing a hand over his brow, Shaw tried to alleviate the tension headache building behind his eyes. "I have a few suspects, but I can't conclusively prove…"

"Then, it's time to move forward. A fresh set of eyes, as it were."

Shaw's head shot up. "With all due respect, sir, this case

isn't exactly black and white. There are a lot of complicated factors that come into play…"

"Don't lecture me on policework, Shaw! I have an entire forensic team trampling my prized Kentucky bluegrass!" The man was almost trembling with rage. "Your record is exemplary, but there have been too many mistakes this time. I want you on administrative leave for the next six weeks. We'll review this decision after that time." He turned, and stomped into the house. As the door closed, Shaw could hear sobs emanating from the interior.

Dumbfounded, the detective stepped back, stumbling down off the porch. He eyed the crime scene, catching Reynolds' eye as he consulted with the coroner. Raising a hand, he quickly walked away from the house, heading down the sidewalk, oblivious to Reynolds' calls to come back. Fumbling in his pocket, Shaw withdrew his cell phone. It was a long shot, calling Lindsay, not knowing her shifts at the hospital.

He was in luck. She answered.

"Linds…what are you up to?" He knew he sounded despondent.

"I was just dropping Taylor off at his friend's house. What's up?"

"I need a ride."

***

Following Shaw's garbled directions, Lindsay pulled into an affluent neighborhood, and down a side street. Shaw was sitting on the curb, his head in his hands. She parked a few feet back and got out.

"Greg?"

When he met her gaze, she could see his eyes were bloodshot. She wrapped an arm around his shoulders, resting her head against him. "Come on. I'll take you home."

Gently guiding him to his feet, Lindsay headed to the

passenger side of the car, opening the door so Greg could get in. "You'll have to give me directions again."

"Yeah…sorry." He coughed, his voice husky, looking like he'd aged twenty years since they had last seen each other. Lines formed around his eyes, as he quietly told her how to get to his house.

Lindsay pulled up outside the suburban home. The grass was overgrown, no doubt neglected thanks to the time Greg was putting in on the case. The interior was much the same. She waited for Greg to take off his coat, as he surveyed the once happy family home.

"I'm sorry. Not been home much."

"It's okay. Umm, coffee?" She started toward what she assumed was the kitchen, when he wrapped an arm around her waist, and pulled her into his arms, burying his face into her neck.

Lindsay recognized when someone needed to be held. Being in the medical profession, she often witnessed how the simple gesture helped many of her patients. Moving her arms around him, they embraced in the hallway.

"They put me on admin leave, Linds," his muffled voice rumbled against her skin.

"How can they do that?"

"They found a body dumped on the chief's lawn…so pretty easily, I guess."

Lindsay loosened her hold on him. "Come on. I can stay as long as you need me." She made her way to the living room, clearing some paperwork aside, and sitting him on the couch. "I think you need to relax for one night. You can figure things out in the morning."

Drawing her into his lap, Shaw brushed a hand over her cheek. "Sorry…I just…"

Lindsay felt her heart begin to race. She knew the man before her had lost a piece of himself in the previous hour, and she wanted nothing more than to comfort him. Greg was a good man, and she felt a tug in her stomach. She liked him, more than Edward. It felt silly—childish, even—that she could get so drawn in by a man, but Greg felt safe.

"Yes?"

Greg didn't say another word. He simply kissed her, and the rest of the world faded away.

28

Reynolds had watched Shaw retreat from the crime scene with some concern. The man had been his mentor these past three months, and he was immensely grateful for all the opportunities which had been afforded to him. He shifted uncomfortably, though, having watched the chief's body language from afar. Still, he was determined to do Shaw proud. Technically, Reynolds wasn't qualified to be running the investigation, but that didn't seem to matter to Espinoza, who continued on about the vic.

"…Male, approximately fifty to sixty years old. Initial observations are a puncture wound to the neck and signs of torture…kid, are you listening?"

Shaking his head, Reynolds hurried to take out his notepad. "Yeah, sorry."

An unmarked car pulled up behind the van and Captain Mancini walked out. He nodded tersely to Reynolds, and continued into the house, shutting the door.

"Kid!" Espinoza stared up from his squatting position.

"Yeah, sorry, sorry."

"Look, I've seen detectives come and go. Some are wrongly accused of misconduct in cases, but I don't think

Shaw'll be one of 'em. Now, come on, kid. Get it together." Espinoza gestured to another crime scene investigator, and together, they turned the body. "Give me an evidence bag."

Reynolds watched as the CSI extracted a wallet from the man's back pocket. With gloved hands, Espinoza opened it. "Mark Bailey. Huh, I was right. Fifty-four years old. Lived on the east side of the city." He bagged the wallet, as Reynolds scribbled down the information.

"Do you think we're looking at the same killer as the mayor and all the other men?" Reynolds knew he had to sink his teeth into any information he could.

"Possible, but without an autopsy, I can't say. However, you may want to talk to the chief. Looks like he has a surveillance system." Espinoza pointed at the roof awning, and Reynolds observed the blinking red light. "Could just be a dummy system, but ya never know. Right, boys, let's bag and tag 'im."

The crime scene techs hoisted the body into a black bag and wheeled it on a gurney to the waiting van.

"I'll let ya know what I find out. Give my regards to Shaw." Espinoza gave a half salute, but Reynolds was already walking toward the chief's residence.

He knocked once, and Mancini opened the door. "Oh, Reynolds. Come in." Before they reached the living room, where the rest of the family sat, Mancini pulled Reynolds to the side. "Look, with Shaw gone, I'll be taking over the case. I know you've put in a lot of man hours, so you can continue to shadow me, but no bullshit, got it?"

Reynolds nodded nervously. "Yes, sir. Uh, sir? Does Captain Brady have surveillance cameras?"

"Really observant, Reynolds. Yes, he does. He's getting us the tapes now. I don't know if the killer is getting sloppy, or if he wanted to be caught." He ushered Reynolds into the living room where a woman sat, her arm around a teenage girl, while another teenager—a boy—lurked in the background, rubbing his eyes and appearing generally grumpy at having to be up at this hour.

"Mrs. Brady? This is Officer…Detective Reynolds. He's been working the case."

Reynolds nodded politely. "Ma'am." He knew apologizing for their presence would probably be met with hostility. "Could I ask your daughter a few questions about this evening, please?"

Mrs. Brady leaned back, and her daughter lifted her head, staring up at Reynolds with teary eyes. "Shayleigh?"

Shayleigh took a tissue, and wiped her eyes. "Sure, I guess."

The boy at the back of the room seemed to jerk to attention at his sister's distress. He came to the back of the couch, giving Reynolds what could only be described at an attempt at a menacing glare. It was then Reynolds noticed a similarity between the Brady children. They were fraternal twins.

Reynolds quickly directed his attention back to his notepad. "About what time did you come home this evening, Miss Brady?"

Shayleigh emitted a loud sniffle. "Around quarter to twelve, maybe? Twelve is my curfew."

"And what happened when you came home?"

"I saw something on the lawn. I thought it was a trash bag or something, you know? It was hard to see in the light. So, I thought some dumb kids had played a prank cause Dad's…ya know…"

Her brother laid a hand on her shoulder. "It's shit. Why would some…" He glanced briefly at his mother. "…sicko leave a body on our lawn? Messed up."

"What did you do when you saw it wasn't a trash bag?"

"Screamed my head off, ran in the house, woke up Daddy, and he called 911." She leaned back against her mom.

Reynolds knew his interview was over. "Thank you, Miss Brady. We're going to be out of here soon."

Mancini walked Reynolds back to the door. "What did Espinoza say?"

"He says the vic is fifty-four-year-old Mark Bailey. I'm gonna head back and run his name through the database. If I can't find any priors, I'll get prints off Espinoza in the morning, and see if he turns up in missing persons."

Mancini nodded. "Good work."

Reynolds turned to head out.

"Reynolds? I am really sorry about Shaw. He's a good detective. Hopefully after all this shitstorm has died down, we can get him back."

"Sir, if it's not too much to ask, why did Chief Brady feel the need to get Shaw off the case?"

Mancini frowned, sweat beading on his tanned skin. "He had a complaint of harassment."

Reynolds felt his throat dry out. "Sir…who…?"

"Bernard Wilks."

Stuffing his notebook in his pocket, Reynolds rubbed his hands on his trousers. "Sir, you do know he was one of Shaw's main suspects, right? He didn't like how the law office had so many connections to the vics."

"I know, Reynolds." Mancini wiped his brow with his sleeve. "I think this law office has more hold over some of our elected officials than we were initially willing to admit. Find something strong to tie these vics conclusively to Wilks…or hell, even Haversham. They could be covering for each other."

Reynolds nodded, appreciative that Mancini had kept up-to-date with the case notes he had meticulously recorded in the file.

"In the meantime, get the board up in my office. We'll go over all the details in the morning. Get some rest, son. It'll be better to look at this with a clear head."

Mancini returned inside, and Reynolds headed to his car. His thoughts were on Shaw. He hoped he'd gotten home okay. This case had consumed his mentor. There were days he had come into the squad room and found Shaw there in the same clothes from the previous day. He knew he was struggling going home to an empty house. If anything, Reynolds was an observant man—it was what gave him his edge in the investigations game—however, there were times he wished he didn't notice the subtle nuances of people's lives. It was just too damned painful.

29

Shaw stretched, his arm falling over Lindsay's sleeping form. A smile settled onto his lips as he watched her, evenly breathing, lost in the unseen realm of dreams. It had been a spontaneous night, each giving and taking something from the other which had long been lost. He had never felt that type of connection with Carol. Sure, they loved each other, enough to have the boys, but there was a spark missing. In Lindsay, he found that, and more.

She rolled over, and her green pools opened, meeting his own blue gaze. "Hey."

"Hey, yourself." Shaw brushed back a strand of blonde hair.

"You okay?"

He chuckled. "Better than I've been in ages." His phone beeped, and he retrieved it from the nightstand. "It's Reynolds."

Lindsay leaned up on an elbow. "What's he have to say?"

"They ID'd the vic on the chief's lawn. Fifty-four-year-old Mark Bailey, from the east side of the city."

"That's generally not a nice area, but some of them are

just families trying to make a living." She rested her head on his chest, and he put an arm around her shoulders.

"True. No details yet. Seems my Cap has taken over the case." Shaw put the phone down with a groan. He felt redundant, a dinosaur heading past its prime, unlike last night, where he had felt like a stallion.

Lindsay cupped his cheek. "It's not true, Greg. You're still a wonderful detective. I've seen all the people you've helped in my years at the hospital. Many of those families would have never had closure, if not for you."

Shaw tugged her over, kissing her lips. "You're my one-woman cheering squad, Linds." He blew out a breath toward the ceiling. "So…"

"So," she laughed, "you're analyzing, aren't you?"

"Yup, can ya blame me?"

Sitting up on the bed, Lindsay stared down at him, her hair tousled around her shoulders. "It doesn't have to be complicated, or we could see where things go."

That recently familiar feeling crept into Shaw's chest. "Really? With an old coot like me?"

She nudged him lightly on the arm. "You're not that old. I think you proved that last night."

Giddiness permeated Shaw's body down to his toes. "Aww, shucks."

Retrieving her jeans from the floor, Lindsay checked her phone. "Mom got Taylor. I'm supposed to meet Edward at his office this afternoon."

Shaw sat up. "I can come with you." His gleeful feeling began to dissipate. That cop instinct began to settle in.

"No, I'll be okay."

"Well, if you don't text me by two, I'm coming after you."

Lindsay smiled at him, her face lighting up the room. "I would expect nothing less. Now, I could use a shower…what about you?" She arched an eyebrow suggestively, and Shaw didn't have to be asked twice, as he tripped out of bed after her into the bathroom.

✶✶✶

Reynolds stepped back, inspecting his handiwork on the white board in Mancini's office. Photographs of each of the vics, along with their name, DOB, and rap sheet lined the top, followed by each of the dump sites. As a sideline, he chronicled the case of Corrine Evans, attached to Dwayne Marshall. He also attached the case of Freddy Jones to the fallen officers from the robbery. He and Shaw had quickly dismissed Jones' death as a revenge killing, although it was easy to see how someone on the department could have played copycat.

Mancini stepped in with two cups of coffee. "Right. Let's see what we've got." He inspected the board. "You said Shaw's main suspect was Wilks?"

"Yeah. He's tied to three of the five vics, but I haven't had time to look into Bailey yet. I'm headed to the coroner's office this afternoon."

"Good, good. Run him through the database ASAP. Now, tell me how each vic is tied to this law office." Mancini hiked a hip up on his desk.

Reynolds cleared his throat. "Uh, well, the first vic, Holzer, was a client, reported missing by the firm. The second, Jones, was connected through his father, Frederick Crawford. The third, Marshall, we found no conclusive connection, and the fourth, Mayor Bridges, had their main legal representation through Wilks and Haversham, and both were at the charity ball where Bridges was murdered."

"Tentative links, at best. Why was Shaw so adamant about them?"

"He didn't like how they brushed off our questions at the initial interview."

"Let's get them in for a second interview, and really lay on the pressure. I want you to go visit Espinoza first, and see what he has on the newest vic. Maybe we can get something from his background."

"Sir…about Shaw…will the chief let him come back?"

Mancini appeared momentarily dejected, as if grappling with all of the world's philosophical questions at once. To Reynolds, it felt as if the man was aging before his eyes, the pressures of too many years on the force, and too many years of seeing one heinous crime after another catching up on him. Would he, one day, succumb to the same thing? Living in the moment seemed to be the lot of a law enforcement officer. Don't think too much on the details, leave the work at the station, but when it involved a partner, a comrade in arms, you couldn't let it be. United together, you would fight to defend them, at all costs. Reynolds felt that way about Shaw.

"Sir?" he repeated with more urgency.

"I don't know, son. In the meantime, we need to solve this so I can start backing his corner. The chief is pissed, you and I both know that. His kids are traumatized. This goes no further, but I'm pretty damned sure he keeps them ignorant about what he did and does, workwise. Anyway, if we solve this, maybe it'll soften him up."

Reynolds nodded, but the relief he was expecting didn't come. "I'll get over to Espinoza."

Mancini gave a curt nod, eyes lowering as he retired to his office, the tension in his body evident.

✶✶✶

Wilks primed the syringe, this time containing a fast-acting sedative, placing it into his desk drawer.

"Zahra! Bring me my coffee, please." Smiling, Wilks reclined back in his chair. "Oh, and when the doctor arrives, please show her straight in."

30

Lindsay stopped at home for a change of clothes before going to meet Edward. Taylor sat on the living room floor, playing with his Legos. She joined him, pulling him into her arms for a hug and a kiss on the forehead. He squirmed and pushed away. "Aww, Mom, there's a big accident again. The man says people died."

"Taylor, that's pretty grim."

"The man in the park said life's not what you expect it to be."

Lindsay frowned. "What man, T?"

His slender shoulders lifted and dropped. "Dunno."

"When I get back, we're going to talk to Mommy's friend about the man, okay?" On impulse, she bundled Taylor into her arms and held him until his resistance dropped, and he snuggled into her. A dark feeling descended over Lindsay, perhaps some foreboding of what might happen that afternoon with Edward. She banished the thoughts, focusing on her budding relationship with Greg. Her mood lightened significantly, and she released Taylor, who went back to his Legos.

She called out a hello to her mother, and went upstairs

to her room. Sunlight was streaming through the lace-edged curtains. Deciding on jeans and a blouse, with her brown ankle boots, Lindsay sat on the bed, and retrieved her phone.

Leaving to meet Edward. Said to go to his office. Free later?

Greg responded almost immediately. *Autopsy then dinner? I could bring over Chinese.*

She smiled. *Sounds great. C U soon.*

Zipping her boots, Lindsay tucked her jeans around them, and went back downstairs. With a final kiss and hug for Taylor, and a shout to her mom about not cooking tonight, she left. The drive to Edward's office was particularly non-eventful. Rush hour traffic hadn't started, so she made good time.

The dour-faced secretary greeted her without much fanfare, hitting the intercom button. "Miss...Dr. Young is here, sir."

The garbled response came thick and fast, almost indecipherable. "Show her in."

The secretary arched a perfectly waxed eyebrow, and gestured emotionlessly to the cracked door down the hallway. "I trust you know where his office is, or do I need to accompany you?"

Lindsay returned the disdain dripping from her lips with an icy stare of her own. "No thank you, I'll manage." Smiling inwardly, she wondered if a curtsy would be pushing it too far. Thankfully, she decided that it was and spun on a heel, moving toward Edward's office.

Pushing the door open, she was surprised to find it dark. "Edward?"

She gasped as the sharp pinprick hit her neck, and strong arms encircled her. She didn't even have time to cry out as the blackness of the room blurred.

***

Reynolds groaned, pressing his palms into his closed eyes.

Normally, he was quite capable of functioning on a couple hours of sleep a night, but the stress of the case was making even that impossible. All this before he'd even been given the proper rank, and while studying for the exams. Tilting his head back, he took a precious few minutes to have a power nap in the front seat of his car, before heading in to see Espinoza about Bailey. He still had to run him through the database, and his head throbbed at the thought of another all-nighter.

Fifteen minutes later, and thanks to the blaring of his phone alarm, Reynolds extracted himself from the driver seat of his car and nearly stumbled into the coroner's office. The smell of formaldehyde hit him like a punch to the gut, and his stomach turned. When was the last time he'd eaten anything? Had to be at least twelve hours. Scrubbing a hand over his stubbled chin, he made another mental note to get food in him. He'd be no use to Shaw if he collapsed from malnutrition.

Espinoza met him at the door to the autopsy suite. "Shit, kid, you look like hell. Sure you want this job?"

Reynolds felt his hackles rise. "What I want is my partner off admin leave. Whatcha got?"

Holding up his hands in surrender, Espinoza guided Reynolds into the cool room. "Prints have been sent for verification that this is Mark Bailey. There'll be a small delay cause of the weekend. You won't be surprised to know he's another vic of our serial. Found the wound in his neck. More extreme torture this time. If I'd guess, I'd say our guy was either showing off, or escalating."

"What, you're a psychologist now?" Reynolds sighed, regretting the words as soon as they left his lips. "Sorry...I'm just really worried about Shaw. He sounded okay when I talked to him this morning, but I dunno..."

"Look, Shaw is a seasoned vet of the force. He's done everything he can to make sure that this case has been followed to the letter. It's not his fault that the chief has a stick up his ass. Don't worry about him. He'll come out glowing, and you'll have your partner back in no time." Espinoza snapped off the gloves, and clapped Reynolds on the back. "Get some food in ya and get some sleep, doctor's orders."

"You deal with dead people," Reynolds responded, glibly.

Espinoza's face broke out into a grin. "Yeah, and I could do with not having another on my hands. Go. Eat, sleep, take a damned shower. You'll have a clearer head for it."

Reynolds waved him off. "One more job to do, and then I can take care of all those things."

Exasperated, Espinoza turned to go back to his corpses. "You flatfoots, all the damned same."

Now it was Reynolds' turn to wave him off. He left the stench of death behind him as he returned to his car. Once he'd determined just who Mark Bailey was, he could maybe move forward with new evidence to consider. As he turned the key, his stomach let out an almighty roar. Shit, maybe Espinoza was right. It wasn't like Bailey was going anywhere. Maybe he had some time to take care of his personal needs first. Like Espinoza had implied, he'd be no good to anyone dead.

***

Shaw's cell phone rang, an unrecognized number on the caller ID. He picked it up anyway, knowing it might be important. "Shaw."

"Detective Gregory Shaw?" The voice on the other end sounded worried, maybe a little frantic.

Straightening in his armchair, where he'd settled in to binge on some Netflix until Lindsay got back, he perked up. "Yes, may I ask who's calling?"

"Yes, umm, my name is Sandra Young, Lindsay's mother?"

"Oh, hello, Mrs. Young."

"Hello…erm…this may be me panicking, but Lindsay was supposed to be home by now. She was meeting someone. She said if I ever had any trouble, I should call you… I'm genuinely worried."

Angling his head back, Shaw peered at the time on the kitchen clock. It was later than he'd expected. "Uh, have you tried her cell?"

"It goes straight to voicemail."

He gritted his teeth, forcing the next words. "What 'bout that guy…uh…Haverwhatsit." He knew the man's name by heart, but he didn't want to appear too forward. "She was with him at the charity ball," he hurried off by means of explanation. Lindsay had said the night before, they would tell her family together, and he didn't want to blow the lid off the pot, so to speak.

"Ah, you see, I don't have his phone number. I tried his office, but it's after hours now."

Shit, so it is. "I'll see what I can do, Mrs. Young. In the meantime, try to stay calm. Maybe she's just been held up with something?"

"I hope so, Detective. I know I'm supposed to wait twenty-four hours…"

"Not true. If you have serious concerns for Linds…Dr. Young's whereabouts, you can report it at any time." He bit his tongue at the near slip. "I'll make some calls, if that's okay?"

"Thank you. Please let me know if you hear anything." The call ended.

Even though Mrs. Young had said she'd tried Lindsay's cell, Shaw did so by rote, not surprised when it went to voicemail, but secretly hoping it wouldn't. He ended the call, and fired off a text to Reynolds.

Linds missing. Think she went to see Haversham. Going to look.

With that, Shaw grabbed his coat, and headed out the door.

***

She was certainly a pretty woman, Wilks had to admit, but there were too many flaws—mostly in her nature and personality. He was a very observant man, and the chemistry she exhibited with the detective—and even with himself as they had danced—was too much to ignore. She would not do for his protégé, no not in the slightest. Her intelligence and beauty were perhaps her only redeeming factors.

Out of simple respect for Edward, Wilks did not take Dr. Young into his specially designed room, but instead to his personal study at home. He bound her wrists and ankles with plastic ties, laying her gently on the couch. The sedative would wear off soon, and he might be able to get some answers from her about the romantic situation between her and Edward. Temptation was not allowed in Wilks' mind, and he knew he would have to dispose of her after he gained the knowledge he desired.

31

Edward checked his watch for the fifth time. Lindsay was late, and her phone kept going to voicemail. He could feel the agitation rising in his chest. Thankfully, he had managed to back up his contacts from his lost phone—technology was a wonder—but when he went to backtrack over the texts, he found they hadn't reappeared. The guy at the Apple store told him it could take a little while, or they might not reappear at all. Incompetence irritated Edward to the core, as did tardiness.

He checked his phone again and jiggled his leg, before giving up entirely. There was no way he was going to wait for someone who didn't consider him a priority. Disappointment flooded him again, as he recalled the night of the charity ball—another moment of abandonment. He stepped out of the coffee shop into the crisp fall air. Thanksgiving was in a week, where families would join together to eat and give gratitude to the blessings of the year. Again, he would spend it alone.

Bitterness swept through him. Wilks had deprived him of a family. Regardless of their faults, they had been his, and he deserved to have had that opportunity to be raised by a mother and a father. Instead, Wilks had taken it upon himself to be judge, jury, and executioner. There was no reason for him to wait any longer for someone who would only let him down. He rose and walked down University Avenue, dodging students and mothers with strollers. As he did, his mind unexpectedly landed on Lindsay's son, Taylor. He had only met the boy once, but his bright, mischievous eyes reflected back to him a time when he, too, carried that same optimism about the world around him.

Despite Wilks' contention, Edward thought he wouldn't mind being a father, yet there was so much evil in the world from which children needed protecting. Lindsay did her best, and she adored her child. When they were together, he had noticed, the room brightened. Again, his feelings on the matter did a 180-degree flip. Perhaps she was simply held up by her son, or something at the hospital? An emergency which required her particular expertise. Yes, optimism did place a lighter spin on things.

Picking up his phone, he dialed her number, which went directly to voicemail, no rings. She would switch off her phone if she was at the hospital. He sighed with audible relief, drawing the stares of some of the people around him. Ignoring them, Edward left a brief message, saying he understood if something had come up, and for her to please call him. All was forgiven. Delighted with this plausible turn of events, he continued his walk, eagerly awaiting Lindsay's return call. Maybe they could spend time with Taylor? There was a park he said he was fond of going to.

***

Wilks sat on a bench at the small park, watching the young boy play, as he spread breadcrumbs for the ducks. His grandmother had a worried look in her eyes, lines furrowing on her forehead as she continually checked her cell phone. Chuckling to himself, he assumed she had realized her daughter was missing. A secret thrill hummed in his chest. He knew exactly where the doctor was. He almost considered speaking to the boy but changed his mind. His grandmother would be on high alert; there was no sense in drawing attention to himself.

Tossing the remaining handful at the quacking waterfowl, Wilks stood, returning to his waiting limousine. Tonight, he would demonstrate to Dr. Young the importance of his work. It meant so much to him that she understood why he was doing this, why Edward's role in his ultimate plan was so crucial, and why she had no place in it whatsoever. It momentarily troubled him to take such an accomplished person away from the medical community. After all, there were so few doctors who maintained the level of empathy Dr. Young did for the poorer elements of the population. He had observed such at the charity ball, her enthusiasm for helping those less fortunate not going unnoticed.

Smiling, Wilks slid into the warm interior of the limousine. The air was turning crisp, although not as chilly as it had been in some of the other places he had lived. Growing up had been a bitter existence. He loathed acknowledging the fact that he came from a cliché. His father was an abusive alcoholic, his mother a cowering submissive fool—the pantomime played out in so many American homes. This may have explained his distaste for men who took advantage of women.

As he stared out the window, the city moving slowly by, Wilks realized he was going to be taking advantage of a woman shortly. Not in a sexual way, oh no, he had no need to exert that sort of controlling power over a female. However, he was going to use a woman for his own gain. Was he so very much like his father? He had considered that psychopathy might run in his genetics. Scientists had failed to prove it, but he was under no illusions about his mental state. He had discovered his true nature at a very young age, and had grown up learning how to conceal it.

Wilks remembered an article a so-called client had sent him, via email. He had been tempted to ignore it, but the title had caught his attention, and even more so, he was curious about a book listed in the content. He had never been one for psychological mumbo-jumbo, despite using the techniques many times to get his clients off on negligible charges, however, he did purchase the book, *Wisdom of Psychopaths* by an Oxford-based psychologist. He mentioned 'functional psychopaths,' stating that lawyers and CEOs were among the most common professions where they were found. Had he morphed from a functional psychopath to an actual psychopathic murderer?

Shaking his head violently, Wilks slammed his hand against the leather seat, grateful that the privacy glass was raised so his driver couldn't see his tantrum. These were the thoughts which plagued him most nights, as he attempted to get to sleep, a symphony droning softly in the background. No, he was an avenging angel. He had avenged many, yes, and would continue to cleanse the city.

Soothed by this thought, he leaned back, feeling the tension dissipate from his body. He had been his mother's avenging angel too. Every night, she would come to the side of his mattress, as he shivered beneath the threadbare blanket, and pray. She prayed for an avenging angel to come and save them from the horrors her husband and his father inflicted daily upon them. His younger self had prayed to be lifted from squalor, and be better than all this.

When he was twelve, his prayers were answered, in a fashion. He came to the stark understanding that God was a deaf entity. To answer his prayers, and those of his mother, he had to take charge. His father had never seen the baseball bat to the head coming.

And neither had his mother.

***

Lindsay came to, groggily aware that she was bound, her cheek resting on supple leather. She moaned, blinking as her eyes came into focus. A fire crackled in the oversized fireplace, the red and orange sparks casting shadows over the walls. The room was ornate, but tasteful, bookcases lining the walls in uniform fashion. A large desk dominated the space, and the chair had its back turned to her.

Licking her parched lips, she tried to move herself to an upright position, but her muscles screamed in protest. How long had she been out? The last thing she remembered was going into Edward's office, then darkness. Her stomach clenched as the gravity of her situation dawned on her. Someone had kidnapped her out of Edward's office, and drugged her with a powerful sedative. Summing up her courage, she drew in a breath.

"Hello?"

Slowly, the chair revolved, much like the Bond villain in *Spectre*—her mother was a huge fan of the spy thriller, although having this happen in real life was not ideal at all.

"Good evening, Dr. Young. I trust you slept well."

She squinted, trying to make out the facial features in the dim firelight. The voice was so familiar, deep and melodic. Her memory flicked back to the charity ball and the masked man she had danced with, but had been unable to identify.

"Who are you, and what do you want?" Her head ached as she tried to make sense of the situation.

"Why, dear Dr. Young, I am offended." The voice changed, and recognition sparked in Lindsay's memory.

"Mr. Wilks? What...what are you doing?"

He stood from the desk, and crept toward her, kneeling by the couch. His face came into focus. "I aim to change the city for the better, my dear. However, I need someone to carry on my legacy. You will be an unfortunate casualty for my cause."

"What cause?" She squirmed, but the plastic ties cut into her wrists, staying her movements.

Wilks smiled, his white teeth glistening. "Why, the greater good. Ridding the city of undesirables. Cleansing it of people who only lend flaws to society."

"But...I'm not..."

He placed a finger over her dry lips. "I know, my dear, but I need Edward to continue my work. The police will get closer and closer—after all, they are not complete idiots, especially your Detective Shaw. I'm quite sure I saw you leave with him the night of the charity function, no?"

Lindsay felt color rise in her cheeks, and she shook her head aggressively to get away from his touch. "What does Edward have to do with any of this? I...I was going to meet him to tell him we were not compatible. This wasn't going to work."

Wilks rocked back on his heels, a perplexed expression crossing his face. "Oh, I see. Hmm, well, this is unfortunate indeed. I cannot simply let you go, so," he shrugged, "I will have to complete what I set out to do. I will show Edward why I need him, and you will be a martyr to my cause. We will keep this little break-up secret between us, hmm?"

Lindsay's heart rate skyrocketed, and she began to thrash again, attempting to free herself. She thought of Taylor, her mother, and Greg, and unwanted tears began to spill. She had wanted to be courageous, use her wits to outsmart her captor, but she knew then things like that only worked in novels and movies. Silently, she willed Greg to figure out what was happening and save her in time, but she held out little hope. Wilks was a determined man.

"Now, now, Doctor, calm down." He withdrew a syringe from his breast pocket. "This will only sting a little bit."

Lindsay opened her mouth to scream, but barely a squeak emerged as the sedative took hold once again.

32

Reynolds glanced at his phone when he woke up, groggy from the fractured sleep. "Shit!" He sat straight up in bed, and scanned the text message from Shaw three times, just to be sure. Punching Shaw's name in the contacts, he paced his bedroom as he waited for an answer. "Come on, come on...shit!" The phone rang out to voicemail.

Tugging on his discarded trousers from the night before, Reynolds yanked on his shirt and shoes, reaching for his keys. The case files he wasn't supposed to bring home, but had all the intentions of continuing to study, rested on a side table. He grabbed them. Just as he hit the door, his phone rang. "Oh, please..." It was Mancini. "Sir?"

"Reynolds, we have a problem."

Thinking Mancini must know about the missing doctor, and Shaw going rogue, he nodded, balancing the phone between his cheek and shoulder. "Yes, sir, I know. Shaw..."

"What about Shaw?"

Reynolds felt his stomach turn. "You...he...you don't know?"

"Spit it out!" He could hear Mancini's temper rising.

"Dr. Young...the one who saw to the mayor at the ball...is missing. Shaw said he was going to look for her."

"Damn it all to hellfire! This is the last thing what we need. Have you tried to call him?"

"First thing I did, sir." Reynolds descended the short flight of stairs to the parking lot of his small apartment complex. He fumbled for his car keys. "I'm on my way in now."

"We have to track Shaw. I'll get the tech guys on it. In the meantime, you go to the law offices. Shaw had a hunch. No doubt he'll think Haversham or Wilks are involved in this mess, and must have taken Dr. Young. Did you know they were that close?"

Reynolds slumped into the driver seat. "I..."

"It's not important now. Get over there, and fast. We can't let this hit the news."

Hitting the gas, Reynolds sped in the direction of the law office. As he slowed on the approach, he noticed a man sitting on the sidewalk outside the building. Drawing closer, he recognized Shaw, head in his hands. He parked the car illegally, and jumped out.

"Sir?"

Shaw lifted his head, eyes black, clothes rumpled. "They're not here. No one can tell me where they are. Useless fuckers."

Reynolds breathed slowly. "We have to get you home. Mancini knows now that Dr. Young was kidnapped..."

"No! I know it was that fucker. I need to know where he lives."

"We have to take this slow. We don't know who is responsible..."

Shaw leapt to his feet, his hand curling around Reynolds' shirt. "It's either Haversham or Wilks. One of those slimy bastards has Linds."

Reynolds placed a hand over Shaw's. "I know, sir, but

without probable cause, we can't get a warrant."

Shaw abruptly released him. "Of course I know that." He paced recklessly up and down the sidewalk. "You have to get me their addresses. Come on...you owe me that much."

Shifting nervously, Reynolds was torn between his loyalty to the man who had taught him so much and his career, which could end before it had even begun. As he opened his mouth to voice his concerns, Shaw cut him off.

"You can't. You're too good, kid." He eyed the younger man up and down. "I could bet money the case files are on your back seat. Am I right?"

Reynolds flicked his eyes, watching the pedestrians passing, their looks betraying mild curiosity at the confrontation. "What are you thinking?"

"Your future, kid. Get in the car." Shaw's hand encircled Reynolds' forearm. "Just do it."

Feeling his stomach knot for the second time that morning, Reynolds obeyed. Shaw quickly got into the passenger seat. "Drive. To the duck pond."

Reynolds put the car in gear and maneuvered out onto the street. His palms began to sweat. Had Shaw taken leave of his senses? What the fuck was going on? The duck pond would be relatively busy, as the weather that morning was clear and warm. Nothing would go unnoticed.

"Pull off here."

Reynolds did as directed, his stomach tightening further. "What's going on, sir?"

Shaw shifted in the seat, facing him. "We're gonna go for a walk." He exited the car. "Come on, kid."

They looked out of place at the duck pond full of happy families. They cut off down a side path, moving into a copse of trees with some dense foliage. Once they were concealed from view, Shaw faced him.

"Look, kid, Linds is the first good thing I've had in a long time. We were starting something special when she went to break up with Haversham. He said to meet her at his office. I don't know what happened from there, but Lindsay's mom called me to say she never came home. Things are so messed up right now, I can't even think straight, but I know either Haversham or Wilks is responsible. In this job, you gotta go with your gut sometimes. Too many coincidences for my liking."

Shaw placed a hand on Reynolds' shoulder. "Here's what's gonna happen. You're going to let me punch you in the face a couple times. You'll probably lose consciousness. When you come to, you're gonna go to a payphone, cause I'm gonna smash your cell, and call the station. You're gonna tell them I accosted you, stole your case files, and your car."

"Sir...it doesn't have to be like this." Reynolds stared into the eyes of his mentor. "We can go..."

"And do what? Wait for a warrant for the security cameras on Wilks' building? Twiddle our thumbs while some psychopath has Lindsay? I can't take a back seat to this one."

Before Reynolds could answer, he saw Shaw's fist speeding toward his face.

***

Whimpers and cries pulled Lindsay back to consciousness. In the center of the study, there was a man bound to a chair. Wilks stood over him, meticulously dripping something from a syringe onto the man's exposed arm. With each drop, the skin sizzled. Lindsay struggled to a seated position, the plastic from the cuffs cutting into her wrists. Her shoulders ached with the exertion.

"Ah, Dr. Young, so good of you to join us."

The restrained man's eyes frantically found hers, begging for some sort of reprieve from the torture.

"This is Brian. He exploits young children for monetary gain. He's also a teacher."

The man shook his head wildly. "No...no..." His winced and thrashed, as more drops fell on his skin.

"Liar, liar, Brian. You know it's so rude." Wilks' expression was maniacal, but with a strange calm in his eyes. "You think people like this deserve to live in our city? To be exposed to children...your son, maybe?"

Lindsay gritted her teeth, unwilling to give Wilks the satisfaction of hearing her thoughts.

"Come now...tell me what you think." Wilks jabbed the syringe into the man's hand, eliciting an ear-piercing wail from his victim.

"I don't know what the hell you're talking about! I work at Target! I've never been a teacher! Please let me go." The man's eyes were streaming with tears.

"Well, Dr. Young?"

She swallowed past the sandpaper feeling in her throat. "I...think the justice system..."

"Yes?" Wilks prompted. "Do continue."

"I think that, while it is flawed, it is better than this form of vigilante behavior. You can't be..."

Wilks strode over and backhanded her. "Liar!"

Her head snapped back, and she tasted the bitter copper flavor of blood where he'd split her lip.

"This is exactly why you would never be a good match for my protégé. You could never understand my true mission. But you will."

Spots swam before Lindsay's eyes as she tried to block out the agonizing screams of the man being tortured before her.

33

Edward crossed the small park next to the duck pond. He didn't know if Lindsay's mother would be there with the young boy, but if he understood anything it was the need to keep things normalized when unexpected events were occurring. Going to the park on a Saturday morning was one of the things done by rote with Taylor. Lindsay had mentioned it briefly on their shopping excursion for the charity ball.

Sure enough, his instincts proved correct. Taylor was playing on the structure while Sandra Young sat nearby, watching him more closely than usual. Her gaze skimmed over him twice before recognition dawned and she stood, casting a final look at Taylor before approaching.

"Where the hell is my Lindsay?"

Edward's brow furrowed. He tugged at the collar of his unbuttoned dress shirt. "I was under the impression she would be here. Doesn't she always bring Taylor when she's off-shift?"

Sandra's hands planted on his chest, giving him a shove. "No, she was meant to be with you. Where is she?"

Sensing the woman's distress and trying to quell his

own building concern, Edward shook his head. "No, you don't understand. She never came. That's why I'm here. I was hoping to see what was wrong. Her phone is going to voicemail."

Sandra quickly checked on Taylor before taking his arm. "I'm not sure I understand what you mean. She said you texted to meet her at the office. I haven't heard from her since."

"I'm sorry, but I never did. I lost my phone, you see…" Edward trailed off, thinking to the last time he had seen his phone. He could only remember having it when he was at Wilks' home that horrible evening… He gasped.

"What?"

"I know where she is, but there's little time. You must call the police and tell them Bernard Wilks has Lindsay." He spun on a heel.

"Where are you going?"

"To confront a madman."

***

The moans of the man in front of Lindsay subsided as he slipped into the blissful arms of insentience. A steady ache built in her chest, compounded with a desire to help—something which, despite the situation, would always be in the forefront of her mind, the need to help others in times of need. Wilks sat at his desk now, puffing on a cigar, the circles of wispy gray smoke like morbid halos.

"I've never done anything to you. Why do you have to do this? How am I even relevant to this twisted shit?" Lindsay's hands felt numb from the cuffs, and she flexed her fingers to try and restore some circulation.

"It's all in the grand plan, my dear."

She all but screamed, "I don't want to be with Edward! We're not compatible. Don't you understand? You could have avoided all this. Now Detective Shaw…" She fumbled over the words. Greg didn't know she was here.

She had only told him she was meeting Edward at a coffee shop near his work. No, Greg was smart, she admonished herself. He'd figure it out.

"The police are mindless bureaucratic puppets. I left two bodies in the same place, and they were oblivious. In the end, the clues in these cases will run dry—no one cares about junkies or those who are little more than boils on the back of society."

She jerked her head in the direction of the unconscious man between them. "And him? He said he doesn't know what you're talking about. Maybe you've lost your touch with the reality of your cause." *Keep him talking. Make it about him. Give Greg time to find me.*

"People lie, Dr. Young. I'm sure you lie all the time to your patients, make promises of recovery which you can never keep. Everybody lies!" He pounded his fist on the polished surface of the desk.

Lindsay frantically tried to recall details from her few psychology classes at college. They were part of the required curriculum, and she had always found the subject fascinating, but working with the mind was too uncertain. She had preferred the factual nature of medicine, piecing together a puzzle was part of the challenge as well.

"Who lied to you?" The question tumbled out before she could filter it. Maybe that was for the best. She didn't have time for hesitation.

"Your diversion tactics are admirable, Dr. Young. I suppose I should be proud you're making some effort…that you still retain some modicum of hope that someone will find you. Very well. My father was abusive. Does that answer those questions whirring away in your brain about my motivations? If you see it as the all-encompassing reason why I do this, you would be wholly incorrect, my dear. I do this to cleanse the city. So that children—like your little boy—can live uncorrupted by this vice."

Lindsay tensed at the mention of Taylor. "But you cannot possibly kill all the people in the city who don't fit your mold. It doesn't make sense."

Wilks rose from behind the desk, strolling towards the gleaming silver tray containing multiple vials and syringes. "Enough discussion. It's time to wake up our friend here."

If only clamping her hands over her ears was an option. The subsequent sounds as the result of the man's enduring torture reverberated in her brain, bouncing off each neuron like a ping pong ball. *Please, Greg…find me in time…*

✱✱✱

"It's a dead body."

"No, you're dumb. He's breathin'. See?"

A sharp jab hit Reynolds right below the ribs.

"I'm gonna get Mom, and you're both gonna get into trouble!"

Reynolds groaned, and clutched his head. A chorus of screams had him wincing, and the pounding and crunching of feet on dirt and leaves faded into the distance. A few moments later, the pounding returned. He could feel the vibrations through the ground.

"Sir? Sir, should I call 911?"

Peeking up through slotted lids, Reynolds made out four blurry figures, three shorter than the one in the middle. His throat felt like someone had dumped sand down it as he rasped, "Yes…"

"What's your name?"

As his vision cleared, he finally focused on the woman dressed sensibly in jeans, a t-shirt, and sneakers, hair pulled back in a utilitarian ponytail—what he would describe as your typical casual mom attire. Surrounding her were three children of various ages, two boys and a girl. Their wide eyes never left him. He must be a sight, with dried blood around his nose and lips. His nose must have been broken, as fiery pain rippled through his face as he tried to speak.

"Detective Nick Reynolds, Palo Alto PD. Ask for Captain Mancini." He rested his head back in the foliage, listening to the hurried tones of the woman as she made the call.

34

The ambulance blared into the parking lot of the duck pond, followed closely by Captain Mancini's car and two squad vehicles. Reynolds had propped himself up on a tree, the woman who had found him, along with her kids, kneeling down beside him. One uniform led the small family away for a brief interview, and the paramedics performed their tasks as Captain Mancini hovered over them, a frown deepening the lines on his face.

"What happened, son?"

In between the ministrations of the EMTs, Reynolds relayed the story concocted by himself and Shaw. "Shaw texted me, said he wanted to talk. He was in a bad place, sir, worried about the cases. He kept going on about Dr. Young, you know, the one who treated the former mayor? Anyway, he said he wanted to come here, and before I knew what was happening, he snapped. Next thing I knew, I'm waking up to some kid poking me in the ribs with a stick." His eyes skimmed the gathered crowd, and one boy looked down. Reynolds managed to crack a half-smile, knowing he'd have done the same thing, if he were the boy's age.

"Where's your car?"

"Parking lot, sir."

Captain Mancini stalked off, directing some officers to control the crowd. The paramedic in charge decided a trip to the hospital was in order, along with some x-rays to determine the extent of the damage to Reynolds' nose and face, and attempted to guide him onto a gurney.

"I can walk, it's fine." Reynolds, with the assistance of the two paramedics, got to his feet as Mancini returned, walking at full speed.

"Were the case files in your car?"

"I was bringing them back to the precinct when Shaw texted me. Why?" Reynolds knew exactly where those files were…and exactly where Shaw would be headed. He wondered if he should drop the act, but maybe there was a way to kill two birds with one stone, so to speak.

"They're gone."

"Shit. Why would he take them?" Reynolds leaned heavily on one of the paramedics. "Damn it."

"What is it? Come on, son, speak up." Panic laced Mancini's voice at this point.

"He kept muttering about Wilks, how he was behind all this. And how Haversham knew about it. I told him I would call it in, but he said he would take care of it himself. Wilks was unstable."

"What would give him that idea? None of this is in his case notes."

The paramedics, impatient with the delays, began directing Reynolds to the waiting ambulance. "We need to get him seen and make sure there's no internal damage," the paramedic in charge said.

Mancini held up a hand. "I understand, but this is an active murder investigation." He faced Reynolds again. "What gave him the idea Wilks would be involved? I thought his beef was with Haversham."

"I don't know, sir, but maybe you can catch him before

he gets there."

"There?"

"He said he would take care of things himself, right before he hit me. I guess that means he's going to talk to Wilks."

***

Shaw pulled up to the dark apartment complex, surprised at the lax security measures for someone as well off as his suspect. Or maybe they were just concealed. His mind was a blur, filled with thoughts of Lindsay, his boys, the case. All he wanted was to have his name back in good standing. *No thanks to the commissioner*, he thought. If only they had listened before when he'd said there was something funny about Haversham.

He double-checked the file, making sure he had the right address, and progressed to the unit. Slamming his fist on the door, he soon determined no one was home. "Fuck!" He hit the door once again, venting his frustrations. *Where the hell could Lindsay be, if not here?* He mentally scrolled through the case notes, things he had noticed during the course of the investigation, and his mind landed on Zahra Hamid, the receptionist from the law firm. Returning to his truck, he opened the file, skimming the list of interviewee names and addresses until he landed on the woman's. She lived not too far from his current location. Perhaps it was time to conduct a more thorough interview of Miss Hamid.

A light glowed from behind dark curtains in the small house listed as Miss Hamid's residence. Shaw wasted no time in knocking on the door. It was opened by the statuesque administrative assistant of Wilks and Haversham. Her dark hair shone, let down from the stern styling he remembered. Her form was draped in a flowing white silk robe and the scent of jasmine infused his senses.

"May I help you?" Her head tipped to the side, in a

coquettish fashion.

Shaw realized he had no badge to show. "Yes, my name is Detective Gregory Shaw and..."

"Oh, the one investigating all those crimes. Do come in."

The apartment was clean with candles glowing. She guided him into the living room where a bottle of wine and two glasses sat on the coffee table.

"I'm sorry. I seem to have interrupted your evening." Shaw turned to leave, but she snagged his arm.

"You are my evening, Detective." She glided a finger down the front of his chest.

What the... "Ma'am, I think there's been a misunderstanding..."

"Oh, no misunderstanding at all! The case must be so stressful..."

Shaw had never considered himself a man who would be violent to women, but there was something about this Jezebel which made his stomach turn. He hadn't seen it before—maybe because he was so fixated on the case—but her predatory eyes raked over him. She pushed him back on the couch, and straddled his lap. He brought his hands up to protest, but she pinned them on either side of his head. Her strength was unexpected for such a lithe woman, but he should have known better than to underestimate any woman.

"Ma'am, I'm asking you as an officer of the law to remove yourself..."

"You're not an officer anymore, are you? Mr. Wilks said you'd been taken off the case."

"Wilks...what does he..." His brain jolted, as if hit by an electric shock. Sure, he had suspected Wilks of dirty dealings, and had said as much to Reynolds, but was he that off the mark—that obsessed with Haversham's attentions to Lindsay—that he had missed what was right in front of him the entire time?

Practicing a move he'd learned in force options class, Shaw broke Zahra's hold on him, flipping her onto her back on the couch.

"Oh, a man who likes to be in charge," she purred.

"Shut up. What do you know?" His hand encircled her neck. He didn't see a woman before him, but a vile viper.

Her eyes bulged, clearly not having expected this shift in power. He lifted his hand just enough for her to speak, containing her wrists with his other hand. "I only know what he tells me. He said you'd come here. He knows people better than they know themselves."

"He must have something on you. Why would you help him like this? He's a killer."

"Ha! He only kills people who deserve it. Do you know what my father used to do to me at night, while my mother slept, knocked out by one of her tablets? He'd come into my room and rape me. Bernard put a stop to that. He saved me. I owe him."

"How many people does this fucker have who owe him?" To Shaw, it was a rhetorical question, but Zahra answered anyway.

"More than you know."

Shaw tightened his grip again, and her face reddened. He released her neck, and she gasped, coughing. "Talk."

"The mayor…Crawford…even Haversham… They all owe him. He's above capture. He has your department running around like headless chickens! No one is going to get in the way of his mission."

"His mission?"

"To wipe the scum of this city off the face of the earth."

Resisting the urge to crush her fine-boned face in his hand, Shaw relented, pulling her up with him. "Come on." He forced her into a dining chair, removing handcuffs from his back pocket. He restrained the woman, who seemed to be more aroused by the situation as it continued.

"Where is Wilks now?"

The robe had gaped open, and Shaw could see she was wearing nothing underneath. He adjusted the material to preserve her modesty, what little there was left of it to be had. "Where?" he shouted again.

This time, her expression turned to fear. "His house, I imagine. He was saying something about forcing Haversham to understand. To understand that he had made mistakes... He would remind him of pain..."

"Pain? He's going to do the same..."

"Pain comes in all forms, Detective. Emotional pain is the worst type. I could heal from my father's assaults, but I will never heal from the stabbing betrayal he inflicted upon me." At that, her face broke, and tears began to stream down. Shaw almost pitied her—almost.

"You could have stopped this. You knew what was going on."

"My father was a respected man of the community. Who would believe me? My mother slapped me hard when I told her. Only Wilks saw through the façade. Only he cared enough!"

Shaw knew his time would be running out. "Does he have Lindsay...Dr. Young?"

Zahra gave an imperceptible nod. "She's his means to an end. He can retire once he makes Edward see. One day, everyone will see."

Shaw was reminded of the women under the spell of Charles Manson, all those years ago. Zahra Hamid was so indebted, so in awe of Bernard Wilks, that she may never be able to see the horrible nature of his crimes. "When I'm through with him, he'll be at the receiving end of the justice he claims to seek."

It started slow, like bubbles popping to the surface of water just as it's about to boil. Her laughter was musical at first, then verged on hysterical. Her face contorted, as if he was the biggest fool she had ever laid eyes on. She truly believed Wilks would be her savior. Shaking his head, Shaw turned.

As he left the half-crying, half-laughing woman in her apartment, shutting the door firmly behind him, Shaw rushed back to his truck. He should call in back-up. He should text Reynolds, but none of those things seemed to matter. If the police came in, it would result in a hostage situation. Wilks wouldn't be taken alive. He had too much pride to be subjected to questioning by the police. He would close up, and the court case could go either way.

Starting the pickup, Shaw pulled out of the complex. Was he as bad as Wilks, seeking justice in this way? He wanted the man dead, Lindsay back in his arms. It didn't matter if he cleared his name now. What was important was having the woman he loved—and after all this time of conversations over hospital coffee, all the smiles and kind words, he did love her. He felt a connection long gone in his own marriage to Carol. He had to make it in time to save her, be the white knight, and bring an end to this, once and for all.

35

The man no longer moved. Lindsay was sure he was dead as his chest remained static. Wilks had injected him in the neck with the hydrochloric acid, and she couldn't watch any longer. Thankfully, he granted her that small mercy. She lay catatonic on the couch, knowing her turn would come. As the minutes ticked by, her hope dwindled. She silently bid farewell to her son, her mother, Greg. She didn't want to die, especially not at the hands of this madman, not in that way.

Wilks pressed his fingers to the opposite side of the man's neck. "Gone. Another blight on society removed."

Lindsay weakly shook her head. "It's...irrational."

"What in life is rational, my dear?" Wilks returned to his desk, observing her with cold eyes. "I doubt your Detective Shaw is so faithful. At this moment, my darling Zahra will have seduced him. Do you want a man so easily led by his baser instincts? Most are, you see, even me. Zahra will help keep Edward in line. She's held him aloft for so long, he'll think it's Christmas when she finally relents."

A cold chill washed over Lindsay and she knew he was

lying, but memories of her ex came flooding back. "Greg would never do that."

"Never say never, my dear. You see..." He glanced to the side. "No, it's not possible. She's never failed me before."

Lindsay sat up, watching as he tapped on an iPad. Hope rekindled, but Wilks merely chuckled. He stood, ripping a strip of tape and affixing it over her mouth. "I suppose when you can't get something done right, you must do it yourself."

Horror crossed her face as Wilks opened a drawer, pulling out a handgun. "We simply do not have time for torture this time, my darling. Shall we invite him in?"

Like an extinguished candle, Lindsay's hope died once more.

***

Reynolds knew his nose was broken before the doctor even showed him the x-ray. Placing his fingers on either side of his nose, the doctor applied pressure and jerked his hands down toward his chin. His nose set with a sickening crack, and Reynolds nearly fainted from the pain. As he held an ice pack to the afflicted area to reduce swelling, his phone vibrated. It was Shaw.

At Wilks house. He has Linds, not Hav. Sorry for the nose. I'll miss you.

Fumbling with his cell, Reynolds knew he should report this to Mancini. They could make it in time to save Shaw and Dr. Young. He punched dial.

"Mancini."

"He's at Wilks' house. Go. Back up. Not much time." Reynolds tried to breathe through the pain.

In a flurry of curse words, Mancini hung up, calling out about a SWAT team and warrants.

Reynolds motioned to a passing nurse. "I need to be released."

"The doctor wants to monitor you for..."

"No, you don't understand. I need to be released. I need to leave."

The nurse frowned. "Do you have someone picking you up?"

"I need..." A wave of pain hit him in the face, and he moaned.

The nurse slowly eased him back. "Rest. The dizziness will pass soon."

Reynolds felt completely helpless. He was letting down his partner. He should be there, helping Shaw, making sure no one got hurt. He picked up his phone, and typed in one word:

Don't.

The response buzzed back after a few seconds:

Too late.

Reynolds gently grasped the nurse's arm again. "Please...I need to borrow your car."

***

The front door was unlocked when Shaw tested the handle. He'd removed his off-duty weapon from the concealed safe underneath his passenger seat, along with a Maglite from his glove compartment. The Sig was oiled, cleaned and ready for use, a reliable firearm, and the means to an end. He crept down the hallway, flashlight beam glowing over the walls, feeling like a character in a horror novel, waiting for something to jump out at him.

A faint light emanated from under one of the doors. Shaw cautiously pushed it open, keeping his eye on the room as it was revealed to him. His eyes landed on Lindsay, bound to the couch, mouth taped, struggling frantically. He didn't see Wilks until two rounds had entered his chest and he slumped to the floor, the wind knocked out of him. He hadn't expected Wilks to have a gun. Rookie mistake. The Sig slipped from his fingers as he pressed a hand to his chest, feeling the blood pump out of him.

He almost laughed at that moment—at the justice system, at the situation, at everything he thought he held on a pedestal. He thought of his kids, his boys, and how they would end up being stoic-faced fixtures as the ten o'clock news covered his funeral, officers lined up alongside the road in dress uniform. Or would they throw him to the wolves? Blame him for the cock-up in the case. He supposed it didn't matter.

He was moving now, being dragged into the room, the door shutting. As Shaw looked to his feet, he could see a streak of blood lining the carpet. *Try to clean that up, asshole.* Small mercies came in the form of Lindsay's hands, pressing to his chest. Wilks must have released her. Compassion, maybe?

"Don't die. Don't die," she repeated in a mantra.

Shaw tried to focus on her face. He could see Wilks behind her, gun to her head, a bemused expression on his features at the futile attempts by Lindsay to stem the bleeding. Shaw reached for the gun, but it wasn't within grasp.

"Linds..." Shaw felt his life slipping away, his breath slowing. "The gun..." His body shuddered and relaxed.

36

Edward heard the gunshots from the foyer before he could make it to the door to the study, and he hastened his steps. He had parked around the block, uncertain if he would make it in time. As he pushed into the room, it was like a scene from one of Dante's Circles of Hell. Wilks stood over the prone form of Lindsay, blood flowing from a wound in her forehead, staining her beautiful blonde hair, eyes fixed at the ceiling, her fingers barely brushing the grip of what he assumed must have been Shaw's gun. Next to her was the body of Detective Shaw, a crimson patch on the front of his shirt. There was also an unknown man, bound to a chair, horrific red lines tracing up and down his bare arms.

He felt bile rising in his throat as his eyes finally landed on Wilks. He stood calmly. "Edward, my boy. You're just in time." He revolved slowly, placing the handgun on the desk. "You can see I've taken care of your problem. You did know she was leaving you for him, correct?"

Edward's arms fell limp at his sides. "I didn't want any of this." He advanced on Wilks. "This…makes no sense. It's completely irrational."

"You wanted the money, the status! Well, this is the cost," Wilks was babbling now, continuing on about debts and cleansing.

"I...wanted to practice law. I wanted to have a nice house, make connections, maybe run for office at some point." He ran his hand over his hair. "This...you're a madman."

Wilks squared up to Edward, and he had to lean back on the desk for support, his hands brushing metal. "You are a fool, boy! As bad as the man tied to that chair. Lack of appreciation for what I've done."

"You took it too far." Edward curled his hand around the grip of the firearm. He'd never shot anything in his life, but he would now, if it meant putting a stop to this. "You've lost sight of your own goals."

"No! No! It's you who doesn't understand. I needed a male. She was too flighty, too unstable..."

Edward looked once more at the bodies. "You will talk your way out of this...find a scapegoat. It's always been your way, Bernard. Well, I think I'm going to have to follow your own advice." He aimed the firearm at Wilks' chest and squeezed the trigger.

Wilks' body recoiled, hitting the floor with a thud as the door to the study swung open. Illuminated in the dim light was Reynolds, the man Edward recognized as Shaw's partner. Sirens could be heard in the distance, as Edward stared helplessly at Reynolds. "He was coming for me..."

"And that's what we'll tell 'em." Reynolds looked forlornly at his former partner. "Come on. We'd better get out of here before the cavalry arrives."

Edward shook his head. "I can't be involved." He aimed again, winging a round off Reynolds' shoulder, and the man stumbled forward against a table, cracking his head on the marble surface, collapsing behind the couch. As the sirens drew closer, he took advantage of the downed officer and whipped Wilks' handkerchief out of his pocket.

He rubbed it over the grip of the firearm, placing it in Wilks' hand. Blue and red reflected off the walls, as Edward opened the secret panel behind the bookcase and fled.

37

The incessant beeping of the hospital monitors brought Reynolds back from the embracing arms of unconsciousness. Strains of classical music, the frantic tempo of a piano echoed in his mind. There was a dull ache in his shoulder, and his head throbbed. Reaching up with his free hand, he probed the bandages encircling his skull.

"Morning, Sleeping Beauty," Mancini spoke, moving around to help Reynolds raise up the bed.

"Shaw...Hav..."

"Shaw was dead when the paramedics got in, as was Dr. Young and Bernard Wilks." Mancini frowned.

"And?"

Mancini placed a *San Francisco Chronicle* in front of Reynolds. "The paper this morning..."

Reynolds blinked away the miasma gathering in his head and began to read. "*Pillar of the Community Caught up in Scandal.* What the...?"

"Keep reading." Mancini's face darkened.

"*Edward Haversham III, one half of the noted law firm, Wilks and Haversham, has been subject to inquiry by the Palo Alto Police Department in their investigation of a series of homicides in the city.*

Despite numerous alibis provided by Haversham, the department refused to let the matter drop. However, late last night, at the residence of his partner, Wilks, the truth was revealed. Who writes this crap?"

"It's the modern age. Gotta hook them in. Go on."

"*Bernard Wilks, in his deluded mental state, was attempting to cleanse the city of 'undesirables' as he called them, leading to the conclusion he must have been responsible for the recent rash of killings. Haversham, wholly unaware of this, gave a statement this morning: 'I am saddened to lose my mentor after all this time. There was no indication of his decline, and I am truly sorry to the families of the people he has hurt by his actions. I will be continuing to run the legal firm, still offering services to the people of our community.' The police commissioner declined to comment, refusing to verify or deny the involvement of Wilks in the unexpected death of Mayor Reginald Bridges at a charity event last month. He did confirm there would be an internal investigation...*" Reynolds let the paper drop to his lap, unable to read any more. "They didn't mention Shaw, did they?"

Mancini shook his head, taking back the paper. He looked as if he wanted to rip it to shreds.

"How did he get all this to the reporter so fast?"

"That's what we are trying to find out, but after they called him last night, the commissioner wanted to wrap this up in a nice, neat package." At that point, Mancini did crumple the paper. "I'm sorry, kid. Shaw was a good detective. Should have never let him be treated like that."

Closing his eyes, Reynolds leaned his head back into the pillows. "What happens now?"

"You take your exams. We get you back to work. As far as anyone knows, you weren't there. Any internal investigation will show how Shaw had a momentary lapse of sanity. It'll all be tied up in red tape. His funeral will be with all the recognition he deserves. His widow and sons are flying out for it."

"What about Dr. Young?"

"We spoke with her mother. Poor woman. And the kid...I dunno. She was in the wrong place. I wish she had called the police, but I guess she thought Shaw was enough. Maybe she didn't know he was on administrative leave. Doesn't matter to rehash the what ifs, though. It's done."

"Should have listened to him. No one did."

"We can only go on tangible evidence, kid. There was nothing on Wilks except a series of coincidences." His cell phone rang. "Mancini." There was a long pause until he finally hung up, appearing as if he was resisting the urge to hurl it across the room.

Reynolds felt his heart sink into his stomach. "What?"

"When you went missing, I was worried it had something to do with Mark Bailey, the most recent vic. Turns out, Wilks had defended him in a case involving child porn a few months back. He worked in a lab which, among other things, kept a steady supply of hydrochloric acid. Recently, according to the lab manager, the supply had been dwindling down on a regular basis. They were just about to question Bailey when he went missing."

"You think he was supplying it to Wilks?"

"Undoubtably."

"And what about Crawford? He had to have been involved in his son's death."

"We have no evidence of that, yet. We need to comb through Wilks' financials. Even then, it's unlikely the rich bastard will have slipped up."

Reynolds glanced up at the TV set in his room. He hadn't noticed it until now; the nurses must have left it on mute. Bernard Wilks' picture flashed across the screen and a rather large commentator came on, his red jowls flopping as he spoke. Fumbling for the controller, he turned up the volume.

"...Maybe we should be grateful for the Bernard Wilkses of the world. After all, he wasn't targeting anyone innocent in the long run."

The female anchor maintained her professional stance. "That may be true, but don't you think it should be up to our criminal justice system to make those decisions?"

"What criminal justice system? We see prime examples here, of men who had committed crimes against society getting off due to good defense work. Wilks proves that. In addition, look at the case of Corrine Evans. Wilks uncovered the true killer after the police missed him right under their noses!"

Reynolds muted the television again. "Is it bad I want to say he's not entirely wrong?"

"Working within the confines of the law has never been easy. However, I'm tempted to revert to Wilks' stance once I find the leak in our department." The police commissioner's photograph flashed next to the commentator. "Turn it up!"

"...Even Commissioner Phillips, who has plans to run for the mayoral office in the next election, agrees with me. I spoke with him earlier in the week, when he revealed information about the investigation not privy to the public."

"That rat bastard. Political aspirations. Endearing himself to the public while making us look like bumbling idiots." Mancini shook his head.

Reynolds experienced something he'd never though he would. His unyielding optimism was quashed in an instant. However, a new feeling rose within him—the staunch desire to right the wrongs of this case. To redeem Shaw, and to fight corruption in his own department. He had always known it existed—to some extent—in all police forces across the country, but this was unacceptable in his own community.

"I have to get back. Shaw's funeral is on Friday. You coming?"

"Yeah, if they release me."

Mancini nodded. "Kid, you did good work. We'll keep

it between us that you let the information slip to Shaw."

Reynolds' mouth gaped open. "How'd you…"

"You're loyal, and Shaw knew that. You'd have given him the information if he asked. He just wanted to save you the hassle of going through any kind of questioning. Don't you think I know? He was my partner before I became Captain. Rest up." Mancini patted Reynolds' leg and left.

Flicking his eyes to the television, Reynolds jammed his finger on the 'off' button. Did Haversham know about Wilks? He must have done. If he'd have come to the police, or gone to Shaw to reveal the information, all of this could have been avoided. In his mind, Haversham was just as guilty, and there would come a day when he would pay for his crimes—pay for the deaths of Shaw and Dr. Young. Reynolds swore to himself—even if it took him as long as he lived—he would get retribution for his fallen partner.

38

Edward decided he would move into Wilks' office, as was befitting the head of the firm. Despite his criminal activity, due to Edward's partial ownership in the legal practice, he had been able to easily buy out any remaining debt left by Wilks, and establish himself as the lead attorney. He would have to hire someone to replace himself, but that would come in good time. The police seemed to have dropped all official inquiries after the news article had been published, and there had even been a formal letter of apology from the police commissioner. He briefly wondered if the younger detective who had accompanied Shaw would pick it up like a dog on a scent, but dismissed the thought. The boy would lose his job at one complaint from him to the high ups.

Zahra pushed the door open with her hip, bringing the alluring aroma of coffee into the office. "Good morning, Mr. Haversham," she purred, setting the tray before him. "You have two appointments today, one being Frederick Crawford. He wants to extend his condolences, and talk about some pressing concerns in regards to his will and finances after the death of his son."

Edward smiled warmly at the woman, old attractions blooming. He rested a hand on her hip. "Thank you, Zahra. Astute, as always."

The statuesque woman returned the smile, and left the room. "I will buzz you when he gets here."

"Thank you. Oh, and Zahra? Let's have lunch to discuss the changes in the firm."

Her golden-tipped lashes lowered demurely. "As you wish." She departed.

Edward grinned, reclining into the cushioned leather chair and closing his eyes. Unexpected images of Lindsay's body flashed in his memory, and he abruptly sat up, heart pounding. She had been intelligent, challenging, kind, but she had been planning to leave him. He felt a stab of anger at this thought, wondering why she would have given up all he could offer. Now, he would never be able to ask, and that irked him on a new level. Still, there was the possibility that Zahra could fill that role. Sure, she wasn't as intelligent, but she increased his status merely with her presence.

And then there was the matter of little Taylor. Despite his insanity, Wilks had provided Edward with a better life, even though he had hoped he would take over his 'work,' as he called it. Still, maybe he could provide for Taylor in a similar way which would bring him some elevation as he grew. Checking his calendar, Edward made a note of the date of Lindsay's funeral. It would be the prime time to approach Lindsay's grieving mother and her orphaned grandson.

In retrospect, Edward considered that Wilks may have been right about many things, and perhaps he should have gone to the police when he had the chance, but—as he had done so throughout his life—Wilks had protected Edward from harm, including the crushing failure he would have felt with Lindsay leaving him.

Edward glanced out the window, and a new feeling rose within him. He may have to wait a few years, but perhaps, just perhaps, he might continue his boss's work. After all, how could you leave something so crucial to the betterment of society unfinished?

***

Reynolds' throat tightened as he watched the coffin being lowered into the grave, the depth seemed consuming and unforgiving. His arm was still elevated in a sling. Alongside him stood Shaw's sons and ex-wife. The Cap and the commissioner were also present, along with scores of officers in full dress uniform. Bagpipes began to play a haunting score, and Reynolds felt the sting of tears in his eyes.

As the crowds cleared, he remained, even when rain befitting the sober mood began to fall. He knelt by the mound of dirt, placing his hand in the moistening sod.

"One day, boss. One day. I'll make it right for you."

Encore

Edward watched as the mist descended on the cemetery. He remained at a distance, hands tucked into his London Fog black trench coat. Figures in black huddled around the graveside, and he could hear the intermittent sobs of the mourners. He could barely make out Taylor, squeezed against his grandmother, the small shoulders hard and resolute. He was reminded of another little boy burying his parents, trying to remain strong in the face of so much heartache. The optimism he had seen in the boy's eyes that day at the park had faded. He would forever be damaged by this.

Wilks had been right. The world was a disgusting place, and horrible things happened all the time to good people, like Lindsay and Detective Shaw. But there were also bad people, and in the end, Wilks had been so consumed by his mission, he had lost sight of the true goal. Taylor, also dealt a crap hand by this life, would see the same reason he did, eventually. There had to be balance in the world. As Wilks had passed on his knowledge and nurtured a young boy, it was time for Edward to do the same. It was time for the next maestro to select his protégé.

Thank you for reading Orchestrating Murder by Heather Osborne

As always, constructive reviews are appreciated!

Please take a moment to review this novel on Amazon or Goodreads.

Acknowledgements

There are so many people who support and encourage me while I'm working through writing a novel. I'd like to thank my editor, Susie Watson—without her, I am just words on a page; Zoe-Ann Killoh, for her help with musical terminology; Julie Cargill and Patricia Rose for their beta reading expertise and finding where I've made inconsistencies; Vinski Laine for his feedback on the random pieces of writing I send him and for reminding me that I am capable; Mark Tilbury for pushing me to publish this.

To the readers and bloggers, thank you for your endless help in promoting my novels.

To my family and friends, especially those at the Angus Writers' Circle. Thank you for continually reminding me that I am sorta good at this writing business.

And finally, to my husband and son, for their patience, understanding, and love.

About the Author

Heather Osborne, an author of crime and historical novels, was born and raised in California. She has a Bachelor of Science in Criminology and Victimology. In 2009, she met her husband and moved to Scotland. Along with her novels and short stories, Heather also has written and directed several plays. In her spare time, she enjoys reading, writing (of course!), and theatre, as well as caring for her young son. Among her published titles are: The Soldier's Secret, a historical romance set during the American Civil War; Bitter Bonds, a tale of black magic in the deep South in the 1840s, and the Rae Hatting Mysteries series.

Find her at: www.heatherosborneauthor.com

Printed in Great Britain
by Amazon